SAFARI

AFRICAN AMERICAN STORIES
parables & tales

DISCARDED

Ginny Knight,
editor and book designer

cover photo by Brenda Gillum
Comet Hale-Bopp among Locust trees
Silver Spring, MD, backyard, March 26, 1997

GUILD PRESS
P.O.Box 22583
Robbinsdale, MN 55422

International Standard Book Number 0-940248-50-6
Library Of Congress Catalog Card Number 98-070462
Copyright © 1998 Guild Press

ALL RIGHTS RESERVED
Reproduction in whole or in part without written permission is prohibited,
except by a reviewer who may quote brief passages in a review.

Printed in the United States of America

CONTENTS

INTRODUCTION - *SAFARI* 1

PHYLLIS W. ALLEN
'MICAYLA'S GATHERING' 3
    'It isn't about the dinner. It's about family.'
'PIANO LESSONS' 8
    'Wasn't long that she was teaching all the Colored and a lot
    of the White children.'
'THE SHOPPING TRIP' 11
    'This meant a two-hour trip from our Ferrin County home
    into downtown Dallas.'

MAURICE W. BRITTS
'JOURNEY INTO REALITY' 16
    'I . . . wanted to show off the town of my roots to my grandson.'
'AN URBAN ENCOUNTER'
    'We've got to do something about our city, our neighborhoods,
    before this mess gets worse.'
'A MARK OF DIGNITY' 22
    'All her life, this was her style.'

JAMES R. BROWN
'THE DANCE GROUP' 24
    'Because I was the only black in my high school, I never
    dated.'

ALEXIS BROOKS DE VITA
'SAFARI' 27
    'My mother's back-to-Africa movement took us to Uganda
    just as Idi Amin Dada prepared a revolution.'

RICHARD F. GILLUM
'MOVING DAY' 31
    'He thought back to June of 1879 when he first set eyes on
    this homestead.'
'THE TELEGRAM' 33
    'The 317th . . . will entrain for duty with the A.E.F. in France
    at 7:30 am, June 7, 1918, from Camp Funston, Kansas.'
'YOU NEVER WOKE ME' 36
    'I'm goin' tonight and I'll find Kansas or somewhere better
    than here.'

HAZEL CLAYTON HARRISON
'AN EXPERIENCE IN COLOR' 38
> 'I will never forget the first time my family went from Ohio back to Georgia on vacation.'

'THE PASSING' 39
> 'My mother was dying and I was totally unprepared.'

LEON KNIGHT
'A STRANGE AND SIMPLE STORY' 43
> 'You know a white girl can't marry a slave.'

'INCIDENT AT THE MALL' 45
> '... one of many stories I could tell you about how I almost didn't live long enough to become a daddy to you.'

'THE THREE OF US' 47
> '... today, how would you like to stay with your grand mother?' The girl's eyes sparkled. 'Oh, can I, Mama?'

MILLER NEWMAN
'JOHNNY REB WAS A BLACK MAN' 53
> 'But this story is ... about what happened long after the war was over.'

'READING DADDY'S WILL' 54
> 'My family began to disintegrate that night.'

GRANT WAYNE
'A WINNER THIS TIME — a parable' 57
> 'I've been out hustled on a couple good ideas before 'cause it took too long to hit the market.'

'THE HYENA-DEMOCRACY' 58
> 'What do antelope who can't read know about juries and trials, anyway?'

'LITTLE RED RIDER FROM THE 'HOOD' 59
> 'But when he showed his big teeth in an un-funny smile, she knew she was in for it.'

NANCY WEBB WILLIAMS
'THE HORSEFLY AND THE BLACK WIDOW SPIDER' 61
> 'Horsefly devised to turn the spider's bad mood into a moment of joy.'

'JOHN LITTLEJOHN AND THE TWO HEAVENS' 62
> 'The hero of our story ... was the best at ... pulling the wool over Ol' Massa's eyes something awful.'

As space permits, notes of interest are included.

INTRODUCTION — *SAFARI*

An Arabic word meaning 'journey' or 'to travel', safari became part of the East African language Swahili. From there, it entered English and eventually came to America. As with many other words, 'safari' itself was on a journey, while still retaining its essential meaning. Thus, *SAFARI* is an appropriate title for this anthology of short prose by and about African Americans. (The metaphor of the name should not need explaining.)

One day at lunch, Dr. Maurice W. Britts, an old friend who teaches African American literature, said that he could use some of the Guild Press short stories in his course, 'if they were only in one book.' Starting with that talk among friends, this anthology is the result.

Over time as the project developed and various titles were added to or withdrawn from the list under consideration, a pattern began to emerge: almost all of the stories are about family or other personal relationships. And even if a story deals with a 'big' issue, such as the conflict between generations within a family or the response to racial bigotry, it does so quietly and with dignity, not violently and grossly. In the process, these stories collectively give the reader a look at American life that is not normally offered by major publishers or the public media.

That's the way we at Guild Press want our view of the world presented. Life for most people is made up of small pieces ... private pieces ... quiet pieces. If that is true for us today, it must have been even more true for the people of our past. And if history belongs to those who tell the stories of history, the varied and talented authors in this collection have a real history to tell — small and quiet stories on a human level.

For most people, the center of life, real life, is people and relationships. The heart of good literature is character and conflict. Those two — character and conflict — work together in a good story to present an issue to be resolved. But the conflict and the response of the character to the conflict do not have to be 'loud' or violent.

For example, in 'The Shopping Trip' by Phyllis W. Allen, Mama Minnie did not throw a firebomb through the department store window in response to racist treatment. That was not Mama Minnie's way of doing things. The response of a little girl to her first humiliating encounter with overt racism is also memorable in 'An Experience In Color' by Hazel Clayton Harrison.

'Urban Encounter' by Maurice W. Britts and 'Incident At The Mall' by Leon Knight both stress the possibility of violence that is often present in the life of a black man in modern America. However, 'You Never Woke Me' by Richard F. Gillum forces us to recall that such a possibility has always been present for a black man in this country. The same story also suggests that the old saying 'You can't run away from your trouble' is not necessarily true. Sometimes, running away is the best thing to do.

In 'Johnny Reb Was A Black Man' by Miller Newman, readers are reminded that many blacks in the Confederate States were free men, not slaves. What about them? The story also shows that even the victims of the evil system could be warm and loving people, as do the stories 'Macayla's Gathering' by

Phyllis W. Allen and 'A Strange And Simple Story' by Leon Knight.

The universal problems of growing up are shown in several stories. For example, 'The Dance Group' by James R. Brown deals with a lone black male in an otherwise all-white high school. 'Safari' by Alexis Brooks De Vita is a coming-of-age story of an American girl in East Africa as she becomes 'African American'.

In the process of putting the anthology together, two things were added that do not necessarily fit the pattern that was emerging. First, Dr. Britts had used the parable 'The Hyena-Democracy' by Grant Wayne in another class, and he thought that it would fit a prose reader for his African American literature course. So it and two other parables by the same author were added.

Finally, we found room for two 'retold tales' by Nancy Webb Williams because such tales were so valuable in the struggle for survival in the days of slavery and reconstruction. 'John Littlejohn And The Two Heavens' illustrates the little rebellions that were going on all of the time, although 'Ol' Massa' probably didn't realize it.

Adding the tales and parables to the short stories completes the vision a sensitive person is able to get, I believe, from *SAFARI*. But, primarily, I hope you personally enjoy the 'journey' as you read it.

Ginny Knight
editor

PHYLLIS W. ALLEN

An award-winning author, Phyllis W. Allen is a life-long resident of Fort Worth, Texas. An account representative for Southwest Bell, she is 'a storyteller' who everyday sees 'people on the streets or incidents that I make into stories in my mind.' A three-time grandmother with one son, she did not publish her first short story until after she attended the 1991 International Black Writers and Artists conference in San Francisco. Then her short story 'The Shopping Trip' won the 1995 Short Fiction Award and was published by the University of North Texas in *KENTE CLOTH : African American Voices in Texas.*

MICAYLA'S GATHERING

Wiping the sweat from her forehead, Aunt Mildred spoke to Micayla, 'You miss the point of this gathering, Micayla. It isn't about the dinner. It's about family.'

'I know, Aunt Mil, but it would be easier if we used a caterer next year. They'll clean up, and it won't cost that much. Look at the time it saves. More time to talk about the old days,' Micayla answered, turning her aunt's nostalgia against her.

Mildred Atkins Patterson stopped her scrubbing and slowly wiped her hands. How could she explain to Micayla that this yearly gathering had started shortly after the Civil War and every generation had faithfully passed it on as a cherished heirloom. Closing her eyes, Mildred started softly recounting the story.

After the war, Great-Grandpa Gus Thomas, a Civil War veteran, walked from Virginia to Texas to find his family. When he got back, his wife and three sons were not on the Jacobs plantation where he'd left them. Amid the destruction, he found several former slaves still there working. They told him that Effie and the boys had headed north shortly after word came that they were free.

For over two years Gus asked every former slave he met about a woman travelling with three boys. He couldn't describe the boys. But he remembered Effie.

Artemus Ambrose, a freedman farmer up near the Texas-Oklahoma border, provided Gus with the first clues of his family. Artemus had stopped in West Texas where Gus was working. Gus asked, 'Ever see a woman with yellow green eyes and three boys travelling with folks headed north?'

A shadow crossed Artemus' face briefly. 'Could be Miss Efiela and her boys.'

With what he learned that day from Artemus Ambrose, Gus drew his wages and headed for the place where Texas and Oklahoma touch. Over a month later, he rode into the lane lined with tiny cabins. In the open common, an old woman was cooking the noonday meal for the younger people working in the fields.

3

'Mornin', maam. Sorry to bother you, but I'm looking for a woman called Effie. May call herself Efiela. Got three sons,' said Gus with his hat in hand.

The woman looked up and said, 'Down the end of the lane. Cabin settin' off by itself.' She bared her smooth pink gums in what passed for a smile, but instead of welcoming Gus, it caused him to shiver in spite of the heat.

The cabins lining the lane were one or two rooms of weathered pine. At the end of the lane, the road curved and dropped slightly. Standing on the porch of the last house, which was larger than the others, was Effie. Gus recognized her immediately, even though she was no longer the girl that he'd left behind.

As Gus walked nearer, Effie turned away from the children she was watching. Her champagne eyes widened and she leaned heavily against the porch railing. One hand reached up to pat her hair, the other went to her chest as if to still her heart.

Gus tipped his hat and bowed. 'Mornin', Miz Effie. How you this mornin'?'

The children stopped playing. One boy about four separated himself from the group of children. Climbing over the railing, the child buried his face in the folds of Effie's skirt. Shyly he peeped out at the man standing in front of his mama.

'Earl Wayne, come out from behind me this minute. You hear me?' Effie said as she sidestepped, leaving the child to face the stranger. Effie gently pushed the child forward. 'This is Mr. Gus Thomas. Your daddy.'

Wide eyed, the child looked at Gus and then at his mama. Confused he again disappeared behind his mama's skirts.

'Effie, you look good. I've been looking for you for a long time. Wasn't 'til Mr. Artemus showed up in West Texas that I had a clue where you was,' said Gus, still trying to get another look at the hidden child.

'Been a long time. Even when Artemus told me about the man he met on his trip, I didn't really believe it was you. Never dreamed you'd come here.'

'Where's Gus Jr. and Clay? They here too?' asked Gus as he looked at the faces of the children watching him.

'Gone out on the water wagon. Gus drives and Clay's the water boy.'

'Jobs like that usually for the owner's boys. How your boys get that job?'

Effie looked beyond Gus and sighed. 'Gus, I thought I'd never see you again. I waited 'til the rider told us we was free. But with Miz Jacobs' still thinking she own us, I took my children to find the freedom Mr. Lincoln promised. Some later, Zebediah, his wife Annie and their boys, me and mine stumbled up on Artemus' place, and he took us in. Zeb and Annie still here too. Right over there,' she said, pointing at a cabin smaller than the house on whose porch Effie was standing.

'Where you live, Effie?'

'Here,' she said, softly. Then she spoke louder. 'Artemus is my husband.'

'I'm yo' husband, Effie. Preacher said so when me and you jumped the broom on Miz Jacobs' place.'

'That was a slavery marriage. This one is legal. Artemus and I have papers from the State of Texas says he is my husband. He takes care of me and our children.'

'Effie, I had to leave. You know that. You agreed.'

'You was a slave. Could have been sold away any time Miz Margie Jacobs decide she wanted to. She woulda done it too. She ain't never forgave the fact that her daddy and mine's the same. She was gonna sell you. I saw the papers.'

'Why would she a sold me? I was the best worker on the place.'

'Cause she saw that you loved me. Saw you work all day in the fields and come home to the babies. Then you come up to the big house just to walk home with me. Drove her mad. Jealousy make folks evil,' Effie said simply.

'Why didn't you come with me? I begged you.'

'I couldn't take them babies and wouldn't leave them. I knew the only chance you had was to go without me.'

'So what we do now?'

'I'm having Artemus' child,' said Effie, patting her thickening waist.

Mildred stopped talking.

Micayla couldn't believe her aunt cut the story off just like that, 'Why did you stop, Aunt Mil? What does that story have to do with the family gathering?'

As Mildred hung up the heavy pot, her sister Jeria approached. 'What are you two talking about? Micayla trying to convince you to let caterers cook next year?'

'Aunt Jeri, what do you know about Grandpa Gus and Grandma Effie? Aunt Mil won't tell what happened after Gus found Effie married to Artemus.'

'Mildred, why you telling Micayla that story? Know it ain't yours to tell. Her Grandma's supposed to tell her the story and pass her that bread-pudding recipe. Micayla, child, you need to go ask Grandma Harriet about this.'

'You know Harriet is not going to tell this child nothing about the Greats. If she told the story in the first place, this child wouldn't be running round now getting on everybody's nerve. You know Harriet has never understood the need for the gathering. She just comes because it's her duty,' said Mildred as she scraped kernels of corn from the freshly picked ears.

'Grandma Frances always said it was because Harriet's daddy left her mama and married Elizabeth,' said Jeria.

Mildred mused, 'You don't think Harriet was going to tell Micayla those 'down south' stories do you? Ever since her mama took her up north, her family roots haven't counted for much.'

Sitting down by Aunt Jeria, Micayla said, 'My grandmother told me, "Who can remember the truth of a hundred and fifty years ago?"'

'Your grandmother means well, honey.' Jeria patted Micayla's hand.

'Yeah, but she never met Grandpa Gus. I did,' Mildred said. 'He was almost ninety when he told us kids how this land come to be Thomas land.'

Aunt Jeria took up the story. 'After Gus Sr. found Effie and his sons, he stayed on at Mr. Artemus Ambrose's place. Did blacksmith work. Gus Sr. didn't talk to Effie much, but spent a lot of time getting to know his sons. On Gus Jr's twelfth birthday, Effie gave birth to a baby girl named Bessie. And as soon as she was able, she too began to follow Gus Sr. around. The next winter a huge snow came and livestock were stranded out in a canyon. Gus Sr., Mr. Artemus and some of the farm hands went out to take food to the cattle. On their way back, Mr. Artemus' horse plunged down a cavern, and Mr. Artemus was killed.

Riding back into the lane with Mr. Artemus' body, Gus Sr. struggled to explain to Effie. Then the screams started and she fell into his arms.

Zeb, his wife Annie and Gus Sr. took turns caring for Effie and the children. Days stretched into months as Effie moved through each day like a zombie. Gus Sr. divided his time between Effie's house and the running of the farm.

One day while Gus Sr. was explaining to Effie about selling her cotton crop, he took her hands in his. 'Effie, Artemus ain't comin' back. You got children alive who need you. You got to choose right now. Either start livin' or you goin' to die.'

Effie's tear-stained face was puffy, her eyes muddy and dull. 'I'm trying, Gus. Seems I'm always losing the person I love. First you and now Artemus.'

'Look at me. I'm right here and ain't goin nowhere,' said Gus Sr. 'And I knows those young'uns need you.'

After that, Effie started getting better. The boys and Bessie helped on the farm, and Effie took over the books. A year later the farm was on a strong financial basis.

Then Gus Sr. bought a small farm next to Effie. 'It's time I was on my own. Thank you for helping me. I'm always right here for you and the kids,' he said.

When Jeria paused, Micayla asked, 'So how did Grandpa Gus get the land? Is this his forty-five acres? I don't understand.'

'Yeah, well, you never will understand with Jeria telling you the Harlequin-romance version of this story,' said Mildred taking up the tale.

'Mama Effie stepped right up running that farm. She worked the fields, cooked, kept house and raised her kids. Grandpa Gus raised purebred stock. The early nineteen hundreds brought money to cattlemen. So Grandpa Gus proposed to buy Effie's land so he could expand his ranch.'

'Though working her farm was hard, Effie fought selling to Grandpa Gus. But when the boys came of age, a portion was sold to Grandpa Gus and the rest divided among the boys. At the birth of their first grandchild, the son of Gus. Jr. and his wife Claire, Grandpa Gus and Mama Effie made peace.'

Effie said to Grandpa Gus, 'We got more between us than most folks that's been married a lifetime. You been saying that you want to be married, and since you don't seem to be able to find another woman willing, I might as well take you.'

Gus Sr. and Effie were married the following Sunday underneath that beautiful oak by the pond. Every year since, we've had a family gathering to celebrate Grandpa Gus and Mama Effie's wedding. More than that, we celebrate family and how we came to be. And each elder is responsible for passing on part of that history. In 1935 when Mama Effie was more than eighty-five, she shared her recipe for caramel cake with her granddaughter and told the story of her life with Grandpa Gus. This recipe is to be passed to grandchildren at family gatherings, but only when they are ready.'

'I started to cry,' said Jeria. 'But Mama Effie said, 'Nothing to cry about, honey. I'm old. I've buried two husbands and your Uncle Clay. I know it won't be long now. Always keep the family gathering alive. Every time you make my cake, I'll be smiling down from up there.' Then Mama Effie pointed to the sky.'

Aunt Jeria paused. 'A month later Mama Effie was dead, buried between Grandpa Gus and Mr. Artemus. The next year was the first time I baked her caramel cake, Mildred made her creamed corn and Aunt Augusta baked butter rolls.'

'Well, we could still get together and tell the stories,' Micayla said. 'A caterer could serve the same menu in a hotel and we could visit without sweating.'

'You haven't heard one word that we said.' Mildred's voice was filled with exasperation. 'This meal is about more than food. Made my first pot of stewed corn when I was thirty. My grandma, Phoebe Thomas-Armstrong, took me aside and told me how her Grandma Sylvia Thomas passed on the recipe after her second heart attack. I've been blessed. Grandma Phoebe's been here to taste my corn for the last five years. Says it keeps getting better and better.'

'I don't like to cook.' said Micayla simply.

'It's your duty, honey. Your grandmother doesn't have any other grands. She's got to give to you what was given to her,' said Mildred.

'What happens if I don't do it?'

Mildred stopped stirring and pointed the spoon at Micayla. 'See this spoon? My grandmother's grandmother used it when she made her first pot of corn when she was only twenty. What will happen if you don't continue the tradition? I don't know, baby. Maybe nothing. But what I do know is that this gathering keeps us connected. Once those strings are loosened, I don't know what will happen.' Mildred looked out at the assembled family-members. Various aunts, uncles and cousins were busy making all the fixings of a wonderful feast as they swapped stories of the past year and years past. The sound of lying and laughter filled the air.

Looking back at Micayla, Mildred added, 'What you make of it is up to you.'

Micayla returned the gaze. This wasn't some slow-talking, backward, verb-splitting country girl. Aunt Mildred was a professional, urban, sophisticated woman of the nineties. But today she was in worn jeans, scuffed loafers and a worn apron, working in the heat thirty miles from the closest jar of moisturizer. And she was enjoying it. Something happened to her down here.

'Mildred! You all over that yakking? We hungry,' Uncle Clay called as he and his grandson Dariel sampled yet another rib.

'I don't know how you can be hungry. You already ate a half of that hog,' answered Aunt Mildred.

Suddenly Micayla realized that it didn't matter what any of them were in their regular lives, down here they were connected sons and daughters of the south. She closed her eyes for a moment. Then she crumpled the bid from Catering by Raphael and threw it in the trash barrel as she walked slowly towards the barbecue grill.

'Uncle Clay, what's the chance of me getting one of those ribs?'

PIANO LESSONS

Every Wednesday at 3:00 my life came to an end for exactly one hour. That was when I appeared at Miz Luvenia Duvall's house for her to cruelly abuse me in the guise of teaching me to play piano. Protests to Mama Minnie, my grandmother, went unacknowledged. Mama Minnie was unrelenting on the issue of my piano lessons.

She had always wanted to take piano lessons as a girl, but since she and her family lived on a tenant farm, she never could. So, Wednesday afternoons I was trapped inside and couldn't play with my friends.

Miz Luvenia lived down by the railroad tracks in a big old house that every child in Ferrin swore was haunted. The house was two stories tall, that alone made it unique in our section of town. There was a large porch that wrapped around three sides of the house, and one whole side of the yard was full of fruit trees, the only ones in Ferrin County not raided by the local children.

'High yellow' were the words used by Mama Minnie to describe Miz Luvenia. But 'ivory' would have been much better — 'old ivory', to be exact, that rich creamy color with just a hint of amber mixed in. Her eyes were topaz with flecks of green and gold. Now I realize they must have been beautiful.

Miz Luvenia was well over six feet and not one ounce of her large frame was anything but well-toned muscle. Her auburn hair was tightly bound in a bun whose size gave credence to the rumor that her hair hung down past her hips. Miz Luvenia was an imposing woman, especially for a nine-year-old reluctant pianist.

Mama Minnie and Miz Luvenia had been friends since they were girls. Mama Minnie said, 'Luvenia was the best looking girl in Ferrin County. All them boys from over in Whitaker used to walk the seven miles one way just for a chance to sit on Mr. Sam's side porch with Luvenia.' It seems that Miz Luvenia ran away with one of the Whitaker County boys to New York City when she was still a girl.

'Bout killed Mr. Sam 'cause he set such a store by that gal,' Mama Minnie said. 'She left with that boy, Charlie Davis. We knew he wasn't no good — too pretty. Can't no good come from a man that looks that good. He can't never love nobody but himself.'

'It was cold. The coldest winter we had ever had here in Ferrin County. So the road was frozen hard as a rock. Charlie Davis was wrapped up in a coat and one of them hats with ear flaps. He had a bundle in his hand. Went right on by my daddy's place, walking and looking back like a man on his way to steal a watermelon. Later that day I was going out to the smokehouse get one of my Daddy's hams for dinner when I looked up the road, and there came Luvenia and Charlie Davis. They were holding hands and walking up that road at a right fast pace, both of them looking back now and then. So it was real obvious that they were not just out for a stroll. I went on back in the house 'cause, like I said, it was the coldest day of the coldest year. Wasn't till church on Sunday that we found out that Charlie Davis had raided somebody's watermelon patch. Mr. Theodore Duvall's patch to be exact, and he had done stole the prize melon, Luvenia.'

Well, the way Mama Minnie told it, Charlie Davis and Miz Luvenia ran off to Harlem, New York. Miz Luvenia was gone for some years before she wrote home saying that Charlie Davis had left her for another woman. Her daddy, Mr. Theodore Samuel Duvall, the most prosperous Colored man in Ferrin County, went to Tyler and boarded the Santa Fe Silver Streak going to New York to bring Miz Luvenia home.

Much later I overheard Mama Minnie telling Mama that there had always been some question about whether the boy that Mr. Sam adopted on that same trip to New York was really an orphan or the illegitimate issue of Miz Luvenia and that roguish Charlie Davis. Didn't seem to matter none, though, 'cause Malcolm, that was the boy's name, was the ruler of that place.

By the time Mama Minnie began punishing me with piano lessons, Malcolm was a full-grown man, and Mr. Sam had been dead almost ten years. When Mr. Sam died, he left all his money and that big old house and land to Malcolm. Mama Minnie said, 'Mr. Sam shoulda known that Malcolm didn't have no man inside that little boy that he was. Soon as Mr. Sam was dead, Malcolm started running into town spending money foolishly on any woman that take up some time with him. If it wasn't for Luvenia, that house and land that Mr. Sam done worked a lifetime for would be gone in the wind.'

They said that Miz Luvenia had never worked one day in a White woman's kitchen, at the cotton fields or even in the classroom like most of the Colored women in Ferrin County. The only thing she'd ever done was be Mr. Sam's daughter and play the piano like a dream.

One day a neatly hand-lettered sign went up in her window — 'Piano Lessons - All Ages - Inquire Within'. Wasn't long that she was teaching all the Colored and a lot of the White children. Even though the two races didn't mix anywhere else in Ferrin County, it wasn't unusual to find a little Black boy and White girl sitting side-by-side on a piano stool in Miz Luvenia's parlor, her ruler dispensing equal vengeance on errant knuckles, Colored or White.

Every Wednesday that the Lord let come saw me trudging down the railroad tracks toward Miz Luvenia's with a worn lesson book in my hand. After the first six months I had more or less resigned myself to the fact that, barring my Mama Minnie disappearing from the face of the earth, I would spend Wednesday afternoons on a piano stool in Miz Luvenia's parlor for the rest of my natural life.

One particularly hot summer day as I climbed the steps to Miz Luvenia's front door, I almost tripped over a barefoot towheaded child that was sitting on the top step. Looking down, I recognized that horrible Todd Parker, whose daddy owned the local store.

In Ferrin County, Colored and White children really didn't have much occasion to mingle. We went to separate schools, churches and even usually walked on the sidewalks at different times. If the White children were on the sidewalks, the Colored children were off them. It was that simple.

Todd Parker, however, was different. He was one of the few White children that we Coloreds had to see on a regular basis. When he wasn't in school, Todd (or Toddy, as his mother called him) worked behind the counter in his father's store.

He would make these really silly faces at the Colored children when we came in with our parents to shop. Then he would wait until his daddy went behind the butcher counter or was waiting on someone in a far corner of the store and shoot spitballs at us. Once he beaned me right between the eyes. Todd Parker was the absolute bane of my existence, and the only revenge I could take against him was to call him our version of his pet name, Toady.

'Hi, Toady.' I beamed as I carefully stepped around the hated Todd Parker.

Miz Luvenia had a standing rule that when a lesson was being conducted you had to wait on the front porch until your turn. Judging by the tortured notes coming through the open window, Clarice Perkins wasn't finished. She was the only one that I knew that played worst than I did.

The dreaded Toady glared at me for calling him by the 'name'. 'You take piano lessons too?' he asked.

'Yep. Didn't know that you did.'

'Just started. My mom decided that I needed to. Sure didn't decide on my own. Don't want to come to this creepy old house with some strange old Auntie hitting me on knuckles like a pickaninny.'

As much as I agreed with him about the creepy house and not wanting to take piano lessons, it just plain made me mad to hear Toady call Miz Luvenia 'Auntie'. And who did he think he was talking about? Pickaninny. I'd give him a 'pickaninny' all right.

I turned to Toady and gave him a practiced evil eye. Mr. Gale Henry said that a man could stop anybody dead in their tracks with the right 'evil eye'.

'Toady, Miz Luvenia been playing piano longer than you and me both been alive. Ain't nothing creepy about her. By the way, whose sister is she, your mama or your daddy?'

Toady Parker just sat on that step looking at me like some kind of idiot. Finally he said, 'Didn't mean nothing by it. Just meant that if I get an afternoon off from the store I don't want to spend it cooped up taking no piano lessons. Anyway my name is Todd. What do you mean . . . is she my mama or my daddy's sister?' Toady was looking genuinely puzzled.

That brought a smile to my lips. 'It just means that you shouldn't be calling her 'Auntie' unless she is. Otherwise, her name is 'Miz' Luvenia.'

Toady smiled, and for the first time I realized that he wasn't really a bad looking boy. That white-colored hair went real nice with those deep blue eyes, and his ears kind of sticking up like that gave him a friendly sort of look.

'I'm sorry. I didn't know that I shouldn't call her that. I always hear my mama and daddy call the Coloreds that come in the store 'Auntie' and 'Uncle'. I guess I never thought about how whether it was right or wrong. Never heard nobody call a Colored woman 'Miz'. But I reckon that if I got to call that woman over in Starlight that runs that saloon 'Miz', then I should call Lu — uh, I mean Miz Luvenia, 'Miz'.' Todd was looking real thoughtful like this was the first time he had ever considered this and it took a lot of getting used to.

If Clarice Perkins had been a better student or if Miz Luvenia hadn't been the type of teacher who refused to let you leave until you had mastered at least one piece, Todd and I would not have had as much time to sit on those steps and talk. But Clarice stunk, and Miz Luvenia was absolutely unrelenting in her quest for excellence. So Todd and I sat for a long time that summer afternoon.

We talked about people and happenings in Ferrin County. Todd asked what it was like to have a daddy in the State Prison Farm.

It was always hard to talk about my daddy, and I had never talked about it with someone who wasn't one of us — Colored, that is. But that afternoon I told Todd, 'He went away before I was born. Sometimes I cry because I don't understand why he had to go away. Mostly I just try to hold on till he gets home. Mama Minnie says that it won't be long before he comes home. Says that the Governor is going to say it's all right — something like excused or something like that. He wouldn't do that if he thought that my daddy really did what they say. Would he?'

'Never,' said Todd solemnly.

It must have only been a little while but it seemed like hours that Todd Parker and I sat sharing the shade of the wide porch steps on that hot summer afternoon. Then Miz Luvenia opened the heavy screen door and called Todd inside.

Clarice Parker walked out the door and made her best crossed-eyes face when she passed Todd. We were back in the real world now. Todd stuck out his tongue, and I smiled a co-conspirator smile to Clarice. Todd went inside, and Clarice started down the railroad tracks toward her house.

Todd and I never really talked again until years later. The Civil Rights battles had been fought and won. We were both adults the day we met in his father's store. I was down from the city for a weekend to visit my mama and daddy. Mama Minnie had been dead for five years and Miz Luvenia at least twice that.

Todd's tow hair had darkened. I now had hips I only dreamed about the last time that we talked. Shyly Todd said, 'Been a long time.'

'Yep. More than twenty years,' I answered.

'How you been?' asked Todd tentatively.

'Been fine, Toady. How about you?'

Todd started to laugh at the dreaded nickname, softened by the passage of time. His laughter seemed to break the ice. All of a sudden the formality disappeared. We brought each other up to date on all that we done over the years. To anyone passing, it was just a chance meeting of two old friends.

THE SHOPPING TRIP

Mama Minnie had a love of hats, especially the intricately beautiful ones found in the Neiman Marcus hat department. This meant a two-hour trip from our Ferrin County home into downtown Dallas. No matter how hard my Uncle Edgar (the driving always fell to him) tried to persuade Mama Minnie that the hats at the local Lloyd's Dry Goods were exactly the same, nothing could deter her from her Neiman's pilgrimage.

Usually, in late August Mama Minnie would come in to breakfast and announce, 'Next week the new fall hats are coming in at Neiman Marcus. Sure would like to go up to Dallas and just look at 'em. Probably, won't buy one this year.'

Mama would roll up her eyes over Mama Minnie's head. Uncle Edgar, who always had his meals with us, would continue to read his morning paper. The only indication that he had indeed heard her was the slight rattle of newspaper as he thought of the all-day trip that this hat was going to cost him.

All that was left was for Mama Minnie to decide which Saturday we were going. Usually it was the Saturday after Labor Day. Mama Minnie always said, 'Won't go nowheres on no holiday. All the fools from hell been let out and drivin' like the bats they are.'

Once the day was settled, the next issue was financing such an expensive passion. Mama Minnie would pull out her leather pouch from her dresser drawer. She would carefully count out the bills and then almost reverently count the coins in an unchanging ritual. First she would count the quarters, then dimes, nickels, and finally the little 'brown boys' — pennies. When she was done totaling the sum of all her counts, she would nod her head with a satisfied smile. Heaven forbid that the count not meet her expectations. If that happened, Uncle Edgar would suddenly get a desire to work for a week or two over in Hancock at the oil refinery. On Friday evening he would come in, kiss Mama Minnie's unlined cheek and place a folded envelope in her hand.

'Boy, what this for?' she would always ask.

'Just thought that some old woman may want a new hat or something.' he would answer, trying to hide his smile.

Uncle Edgar's money added to what she had stored away always resulted in the last stage of the plan.

Early, before the sun was up over the trees, we would pile into the cab of Uncle Edgar's formerly blue, now rusted, pickup truck. Our carefully packed lunch would be stowed in the little area behind the seat. Mama would stand in the kitchen door, towel tucked in the waist of her apron, waving at us as we backed out of the yard.

The trip had been planned with precision. My best dress would be crisply starched and ironed. My hair would be freshly washed and pressed the day before. Mama Minnie had one Neiman Marcus dress — its origins were unknown — that was worn only on hat-shopping trips. Along with her dress, Mama Minnie would wear freshly polished high-heeled pumps, stockings whose seams were ruler straight, and last year's hat.

Uncle Edgar's overalls had given way to his Sunday deacon suit and hightop 'old man' comforts. More than the drive, Uncle Edgar hated getting dressed up in his fancy clothes. 'Mama, why in name of all that's good do I have to put on my Sunday best when l ain't the one goin' shoppin'? Only going to sit in the truck anyways.'

'Edgar Lee. Won't have you shamin' me at Neiman Marcus lookin' like some field hand.'

Mama Minnie's and Uncle Edgar's conversation during the entire two-hour drive was of persons or families who lived or had previously lived in the small unpainted cabins that lined the highway. Mama Minnie would always start, 'Edgar Lee, wonder what ever happen to . . . ?'

I would ride with my face hanging out the window, catching the fall-cooled morning air. Mama Minnie often admonished, 'Girl, keep your body parts in this truck ' fore one of them diesels come by and slice them off,' But I still kept trying to see as much of where we were going as I could.

For any of us to leave the farm was a rare occurrence. I was pretty much confined to the fields of our farm and downtown Elm Grove on Saturdays. This was a real adventure as I saw it. And I was sure that Dallas was the biggest city in the entire world. The first time I'd ever seen an elevator, escalator, or television set was all tied to Dallas.

When we got into downtown Dallas, Uncle Edgar always pulled the mud-crusted work-truck right up into the lane where the jacketed parking attendants were bowing to white-gloved matrons in shiny Cadillacs. The attendants always looked puzzled at us before one would say, 'Deliveries are down in the back.'

But Uncle Edgar hauled his six-five frame from the pickup and walked around to let Mama Minnie and me out. He held the door open just like the attendants had done for the Cadillac women. I stepped out first. Mama Minnie, ramrod straight, walked by the attendants without a backward glance. Uncle Edgar then hopped back into the pickup and say to no one in particular, 'Got me a meeting over in the Ellum.'

Meet-up arrangements had already been decided. Mama Minnie had two hours before she was to be standing at the sidewalk where Uncle Edgar would pull up and, with a flourish, take her newly purchased hat, stow it in the back, and usher us back into the pickup.

Entering Neiman Marcus was like entering another world. There were counters of perfumes and cosmetics that scented the air. Black-smocked white women, who stood guard over these aromatic treasures, watched Mama Minnie and me with an air of practiced indifference.

Mama Minnie grabbed my hand into her snowy cotton-gloved one and walked determinedly toward the hat department. As we approached the hats, Mama Minnie's eyes started to scan the aisles, searching out the little old pink-haired lady who normally helped her. But there was no Mrs. Smythe anywhere. When she stopped in front of a display of soft felt hats, a young blonde woman approached. 'Yes, can I help you?' she asked with a tone that implied there was absolutely nothing she could do for us.

'Yes, ma'am,' Mama Minnie said. 'Looking for a hat. Come ever year to buy me a hat for the winter. Kinda had my heart set on one of them felt ones with a feather this year.'

'I am not sure that we at Neiman Marcus have what you are looking for. Have you tried Stein's Hats down the street?'

'No, ma'am. Certainly haven't. Mr, Stein has right nice everyday hats. But I'm looking for something for Sundays. Likes this one right here,' said Mama Minnie, reaching out to pick up a beautiful emerald-green felt hat.

Before her hand could touch the buttery soft felt, the saleslady removed it from the mannequin's head. 'I'm sorry, but we don't allow YOU people to try on hats. The grease, you know,' she said, as if Mama Minnie should agree with her.

Mama Minnie straightened her already erect posture. 'Where is Miz Smythe? She been selling me hats for nearly ten years.'

'Mrs. Smythe has retired. I am now the manager of the hat department, and our policy is that if one of you want a hat, simply select it, and I will have someone wrap it. But you may not try on any of our hats. Is this the one that you want?' She was holding the hat by two fingers away from her body as if, because Mama Minnie may buy it, it had become contaminated.

I'd never before seen the change that came over Mama Minnie's face. Her chin quivered, but her eyes were flashing jagged-edged sparks of fire. Clasping my hand so tightly that the blood stopped flowing, she squeezed her eyes to prevent the sparkly tears that were gathering in the corners from escaping. 'Thank you, no. On second thought there is nothing here that I would like.'

As we started back across the cool marble floor, I double-timed my steps trying to keep up with Mama Minnie. When we reached the door, Mama Minnie turned and took one last longing look back at the hat department Then she stepped through the revolving door.

'Mama Minnie, you not getting your hat? We came all the way from Ferrin County for that hat. What's wrong?'

'Buying that hat is foolishness. Been foolishness for a long time, but I guess my pride in having every woman at Elm Grove Baptist Church envy me made me commit that sin. The Good Lord knows that when you prideful a fall is comin'. Guess I just got mine,' she said, her voice full of resignation.

'Why wouldn't that lady let you try on your hat?'

'Hadn't realized 'til today that I ain't never tried on a hat in that store. It's jes that Miz Smythe made it like that was my choice. I come in she already gots two or three hats held back in a box. I looks at 'em and she keep talkin' and talkin' 'til I make a decision based on her puttin' it on her head and tellin' me, "I knew that this was you when I saw it. See how good it looks on." Onliest difference is today I come face first up against the rules. Guess for a while I forgot.' The tears streaked her cheek as we stood on the sun-warmed sidewalk.

Almost a full two hours later, Uncle Edgar's battered pickup turned the corner. He pulled to the curb and, looking puzzled, got out of the truck. The whitened tear tracks on Mama Minnie's smooth chocolate cheeks seemed to stop him. 'Ever thing okay, Mama?'

'Yeah, Baby, everything fine. Me and the little one just decided that we ain't in the mood to shop for hats today. Don't know why I thought I'd find anything in that store anyways.'

As Uncle Edgar held Mama Minnie's elbow while she climbed up into the pickup, I noticed that Mama Minnie was aging. Her hair was much more salt than the beloved pepper that she used to claim. But finally getting herself comfortably settled in the truck, she took one last look at the Neiman Marcus store and turned on the cold stony stare that was as unwavering as it was on a picture taken with my Grandpa Bill over a quarter century before.

The trip home was quiet and full of unasked questions. When we arrived home, Mama Minnie climbed down and went straight to her room. She ignored the telegraphed looks that passed between Uncle Edgar and my mama.

In the room that we shared, her shoes were removed and carefully wiped and placed in their box. The seamed nylon stockings were folded together and replaced by cotton ones. Her gloves were carefully smoothed and placed in their own spot in the drawer. The only items left were her last year's hat and her Neiman Marcus dress. Both were removed and lay on the floor in a heap. Quietly she reached up into the dark recesses of the closet and removed her treasure of Neiman Marcus hat boxes and dropped them on the floor in the heap of dress and hat.

As I prepared for bed that evening, tired from the long trip and longer day, I could see through the muslin-covered window the dull glow of the fire out in the trash barrel. Raising up on one elbow I puzzled over the source of the glow. Nobody burned trash but Uncle Edgar, and only once a month. I didn't realize that I had dozed off until I felt the mattress sag as Mama Minnie eased into the bed. As I turned over to face her, the scent of smoke pricked at my nostrils.

The next morning when I went out to dump the day's garbage and saw an unburned scrap of bright red felt, I realized what the fire had been.

NOTE 1 - BLACK SOLDIERS IN THE CIVIL WAR

The 54th Massachusetts Volunteer Infantry, made famous in the movie *GLORY*, has the reputation of being the nation's first all-black regiment. It was formed shortly after President Lincoln issued the 'final' Emancipation Proclamation on January 1, 1863. (The 'preliminary proclamation' the previous September was really Lincoln's last major attempt at compromise as it would not have freed the slaves in any confederate state that ceased its rebellion and rejoined the Union. Of course, no rebel state accepted that offer.)

But the 'honor of being first' really goes to the 1st South Carolina Volunteer Regiment formed (probably in advance of official policy) in May of 1862 by General David Hunter, commander of the Department of the South. When some congressmen (still hoping to end the rebellion by compromise) challenged General Hunter's right to form a regiment of 'fugitive slaves', he responded that he had a 'fine regiment of persons whose late masters are 'fugitive rebels'.'

Several battles, most notably at Port Hudson, Louisiana, on May 27, 1863, and Milliken's Bend, Louisiana, on June 7, 1863, were fought and won by African American soldiers before the 54th Massachusetts made its heroic and largely suicidal charge on Fort Wager, South Carolina, on July 18, 1863.

Overall, approximately 180,000 African Americans bore arms in the Union army, including at least sixteen who earned the Medal of Honor and 38,000 who lost their lives.

Ironically, the first African Americans who took up arms during the Civil War were in the Confederate army, although they were free men, not slaves. Many were wealthy landowners, including some who owned slaves themselves, from South Carolina or Louisiana. By November of 1861, a company of fourteen hundred free African Americans were with the Confederate troops in New Orleans.

MAURICE W. BRITTS

Dr. Maurice W. Britts teaches African American Literature at Metropolitan State University in the Twin Cities. A former councilman in Brooklyn Center, Minnesota, he was the first African American to be elected to any city council in the Twin Cities area. The father of nine, including eight who have earned college degrees, he has edited several anthologies of poetry and authored four books — scholarly, popular history and poetry. His latest book of poetry is *I WILL SURVIVE* (1982). He was also one of ten poets in *BLACK MEN STILL SINGING* (1990).

JOURNEY INTO REALITY

'Hey, this way, boys. You all have to sit in the balcony!'

The words seemed to come from the past. Sending shock waves through me destroying my confidence in front of my grandson. I was so sure things had changed in this sleepy southern town. Now, this!

My daughter, her husband and their son were visiting us from Minneapolis. Needless to say, we were overjoyed when their jet landed. So, when they appeared in the doorway of the plane, we could not contain ourselves. We waved and shouted in their direction. On seeing us, they returned the greeting and hurried to where we stood.

After many hugs and kisses we piled into my Lincoln and headed home. On the way, my wife asked if they were hungry and indicated that she would fix something when we arrived at our house. My daughter suggested that we drive by McDonalds and pick up some hamburgers instead of spending time in the kitchen. Enthusiastically, my grandson seconded the motion. That evening we dined on Big Macs and chocolate milk shakes.

The next day was a hot, humid, typical summer day in Casper. After we finished a traditional Sunday meal, I, a dutiful grandfather, wanted to show off the town of my roots to my grandson.

So, he and I took a little walk through the town, which ended all too soon at the local theater. When he saw the movie that was playing, he insisted we see it. I hadn't attended a movie in years. Other forms of entertainment consume my time now that I'm older.

Finally, I acquiesced and purchased the tickets. The girl in the booth took my money and pressed one of the several buttons on the metal slab in front of her. Out popped two tickets. I grabbed them and hurriedly followed my grandson who was merrily skipping toward the door leading to the downstairs of the theater.

Then, the age old curt reminder. The harsh hostility in that voice reminded me of the same tone I experienced forty years before when I returned unscarred from the war.

All through that war, I felt a part of my past had been sliced from my life. So, when I returned, I had an overwhelming desire to relive some of the exciting thrills of my boyhood.

When the train had ground to a stop a few days before, I had felt good as I stepped onto the Casper station platform. My mother and father were waiting with smiles and waves. I rushed to them and gathered them in my arms. My brown eyes gleamed as I whispered, 'I'm home, mom, dad. I'm home!'

My mother reached out and ran her hand lightly down my dark, ruddy cheek. 'Thank God! Let me look at you, son,' she said and backed away a few steps. Square-jawed, I snapped to attention. 'My what a striking figure you are in that army uniform. So tall, rugged and broad shouldered. You look so handsome, son.' For several seconds I stood proud and tall, letting my parents bask in their pride. Finally, my father put his hand on my uniformed shoulder. 'It's good you're home, son.' He smiled, and I saw a tear in the corner of his eye.

Now, as I walked toward the local theater in the customary quiet of Sunday afternoon, I was thinking about the town and its people. On the surface nothing seemed to have changed.

Although I was back to the calm and peacefulness of home, trying to reweave the threads from the past that had been broken by the war, I felt deep inside something was wrong. I was home again, after being away for what had seemed a very long time, but I felt like an alien invading the town of Casper.

I was well aware that I could not become a boy again. But maybe, by indulging in a childhood whim, I could recapture a little of the mood of my youth. For as long as I could remember, after a Sunday dinner of oven brown chicken, candied yams, Irish potatoes, peas, lettuce and tomato salad, topped off with blueberry cobbler, the children of the town would hurry off to the movies. As in the past, I had eaten Sunday dinner with my family and was now on my way to spend a pleasant afternoon at the picture show.

As I sauntered along, to my pleasant surprise, I found that some of the old joy was still there in the town. A horn honked in the distance and sent a friendly tingle down my spine. A group of laughing children on their way to the theater skipped along, and I felt a warm sensation spread through my chest.

Feeling nostalgic, I took the well worn path through the town cemetery and stopped for a moment at the monument to the town hero. I scanned the towering bronze statue and let my eyes rest on the eagles perched on the pillars at each side. Then, I focused my eyes on the base of the monument and read the inscription:

> Whether on scaffold high
> Or in the battle's van,
> The fittest place for man to die
> Is where he dies for man.

Yes, they were still there, the same words, the lettering a little weatherworn, but there nevertheless, just as I had memorized them at an earlier time. I recalled a bitter night in Normandy when I thought all hope was gone. I had been ordered from my job in the mess hall, where most Blacks had been assigned, and handed a gun. From that moment on, I was part of the Red Ball express. I remembered how, when I had recited those words, a strange peace had settled over me.

I turned from the monument and looked around me. In the distance I could see the Mississippi river, and on the opposite bank I could see the diminutive figures of people fishing. A flood of memories rushed upon me. Hadn't I fished with my father on the bank like those people? Weren't the annals of the town written around that body of water? Hadn't the heroes, the legends, and the town itself gained impetus from those mighty waters?

I stood at the foot of the statue looking over the town, as thoughts of the Saturday afternoon excursions up the river, with my father, passed through my memory. I remembered some of the legends he told me as we stood on the deck of the boat. He told of an ugly creature with long antlers soaring through the afternoon mist with a young brave mercilessly clutched in his claws. And on the ground, a tribe of Cahokia standing in horror as the bird zoomed higher and higher into the sun. We could almost hear the old squaw scream as she rushed off into the surrounding woods to wail and lament the loss of her first born.

My thoughts were brought back to the present as the sound of an outboard motor in the distance. I could see a small boat, its passengers barely visible at this distance, but the sound of their laughing came to me across the water, and I thought of the fun they must be having.

I took another quick glance at the town hero and walked briskly down the concrete steps leading from the base of the monument. My spirit was now strangely at rest. I felt like patting myself on the back at having heroed myself from the grasp of some unknown danger.

'It's good to be home.' I mumbled and headed toward the theater.

A block from my goal, I stopped to watch a group of youngsters playing marbles in a vacant lot. A chubby curly-headed boy of about eleven was on his knees taking aim, while four others crowded around a ring of shiny glass objects. The chubby boy projected an object from between his fingers at those in the ring.

'He shoots connie thumb,' one of the youngsters shouted.

'Yea, hey, connie thumb,' another teased. I wanted to put a stop to this razzing, but I remembered my childhood and how the other kids had teased me. 'Kid stuff,' I muttered and walked on in the direction of the theater.

At the ticket window, with a broad cheery smile, I responded, 'One ticket, please.' when asked 'How many?' by the sullen faced blonde in the ticket booth. Stone-faced, the cashier passed me my ticket and change for the ten-dollar bill through the opening of her cage.

Inside, I handed my ticket to the ticket taker. Unsmiling, the man took my ticket. In a single violent motion, he tore the ticket in half. 'To the right, up the stairs to the balcony.' he snarled, shoving a torn ticket in my face.

I recoiled slightly at the hostility. Stammering, I voiced, 'But, I don't want the balcony. I want downstairs where I can see the picture better.'

'Your kind don't sit downstairs,' the ticket taker snapped.

'But, I served overseas to protect this country!' I insisted.

'So!' The look on the man's face was cold and impersonal. 'You're not overseas now, boy. You're here. Better learn your place before someone has to teach it to you. Now, git, you're blocking the way for these kind folk!' His face lit up in a smile toward the people behind me. Their cherry-colored faces returned the smile.

Crestfallen, I took the ticket stub and stumbled toward the stairs.

Now, forty years later, remembering that bitter incident, I grabbed my enthusiastic grandson's hand. He looked up at me and cried, 'But I want to sit down front downstairs. I can see the picture better!'

I held his hand tight. He kept tugging at it, screaming about seeing the picture better.

'There's no room downstairs. If you want to see the picture, you'll have to sit in the balcony!' the ticket taker growled.

Brushing away the mist that began to form in my eyes, I literally dragged my grandson toward the balcony. Looking back, I saw the ticket taker admit a group of four white youth to the downstairs area. All the while I kept thinking, 'Home! The more things change, the more they seem to stay the same!'

AN URBAN ENCOUNTER

'Roscoe, a City in Racial Turmoil!' These headlines printed in big black bold type leaped out from the newspaper at the crowd assembled.

'We've got to do something about our city, our neighborhoods. before this mess gets worse,' shouted the platform speaker, pointing at the headlines in the paper he held high above his head. 'We've got to do something. The city's becoming an armed camp. Neighborhoods are arming against neighborhoods. Decent folks are afraid to go out after dark. Did I say after dark? Why, hell, they're afraid to walk the streets of this city in the daytime, let alone at night. People are afraid to drive through certain neighborhoods even to and from work. Nothin's safe in this town. Why, people don't want to ride the buses and subways anymore.' The speaker paused to see the effect his words were having on the fifty or so persons assembled.

I sat listening, but not really hearing. This was an echo of lingering panic stampeding throughout Roscoe. The city really wasn't safe. Everyone knew that. And this speaker, like all speakers, was telling us what we knew but, as usual, giving no answers. I knew at the end he'd offer a bandage, no cure.

'I gotta go,' I whispered to my neighbor. 'I wish he'd hurry up with the punch line. It's getting late and I have to drive through the Falcon Hills area to get home. I live on the South side.'

'I know what you mean. That Falcon Hills area has some mean folk livin' there,' my slightly greying neighbor responded. 'We all know he's right, but what's the solution? Hell, them folks in Falcon Hills are so prejudiced that Santa Claus himself tiptoes through that section at Christmas time.'

'I know!' I laughed. 'But the solution is in us Black folks joining with the White folks and getting along. There are some good white folks, you know.'

'Too simplistic! I know it's basic to the solution.' He paused a second, scratched the top of his head. 'But there's more to it than that, I figure.'

Our conversation ceased as we listened to the speaker again.

'I could repeat incident after incident in this city. You've heard many. The point is, Blacks of African descent, we've got a problem and it's up to us as well as the White folks who want to do something about it.' The short, dark-complected man glanced at his watch and then abruptly concluded. 'I'll stop there. I've kept you too long as it is. If you have any questions, maybe I can ask your indulgence for just a little longer and answer them.'

No one raised a hand. It was obvious the people wanted to leave. The hour was late. Seeing no questions to field, the speaker sat down at the head table and took a sip of water. The master-of-ceremonies stepped to the podium.

'Well, now, if there are no questions . . . ' A polite pause. 'Then that concludes our program. Maybe some of you would like to interrogate our speaker after we adjourn.' Another polite pause. 'If these is no further business, then, this winds up our meeting of concerned citizens.'

A nervous sigh of relief emitted audibly from several of the group.

Outside, a light snow was falling when I emerged from the Club. By the looks of the snow piled on top of my car, it had been snowing for quite some time. As I headed my Impala toward the South side, the white powder formed into a slippery glaze under the wheels of my car. Good food and too much wine simmered within me, causing a comfortable feeling in the pit of my stomach.

The street lights on the roadway seemed more brightly illuminated, amplified through reflections from the myriad of snowflakes descending from the gathering darkness above the city. The streets were veiled in white. The line of separation between the street and grass abutting the curb disappeared in the steadily accumulating snow. Only a trace now and then as my car moved forward gave testimony that a roadway existed. I felt like an intruder muscling through the silently falling snowflakes.

Suddenly a stoplight loomed ahead. Reacting slowly, I brought the car to a halt halfway through the intersection, sending a slight nervous numbness through my veins. My body shuddered. 'Gotta get hold of myself . . . the street's slippery,' I mumbled aloud.

The light changed to a cheery green flash. I gunned the engine. The car responded slowly. The rear wheels spun, caught, and moved the vehicle forward. As I cruised along the street, I became acutely aware that I was following too closely behind a tan Cadillac. Before I realized it, the car began to slow. A little slow, I pushed on the brake. Nothing happened! I didn't stop! My momentum continued. The car was sliding.

Ahead of me, I saw the Cadillac come to a full stop short of the intersection. I pushed harder on the brake. The forward momentum slackened a little. Not enough. Like a slow motion silent scene, my Impala clipped into the rear of the Cadillac. The only sound in the white stillness was metal on metal.

For a brief eternity, the street was silent. Silent like the snow flakes descending gently to the earth.

'Damn! I've gone and done it now,' I exclaimed.

'You're damned right you have! God damn it, look what you've done to my rear end!' The occupant of the Cadillac, in a flash, was standing in the falling snow inspecting the damage. He was white, fiftyish and slight of build. He wore a light grey trench coat with a red and blue checkered English-style cap.

Then, from nowhere, as we faced each other, people began to congregate around the accident. I scanned the faces of the people assembling and felt the steady gaze of hostile eyes. Suddenly I became conscious that I was standing at an intersection in Falcon Hills. I was on foot at night in the most dangerous part of Roscoe. In an instant, the warm glow from the wine and good food left me, and my head became strangely clear.

'Are you going to take that from that Niggra?' someone in the crowd shouted.

'We oughta string the bastard up! He can't drive. Shouldn't be on the street,' another chimed in.

'Give 'em an inch and they'll destroy all our property. The no-good Black bastards!' rent the air from the opposite side of the cars.

The man from the Cadillac became conscious of my color seemingly for the first time. His face flushed, His brow knitted.

'We oughtn't let Niggras drive the streets. They're a menace. I don't know where they get the intelligence to think about driving,' a voice in the crowd exclaimed. By this time, a good-sized crowd, mob-style, had gathered. The man from the Cadillac was obviously upset. He looked over the people and then glared at me for a minute.

I thought I saw the hostility and hate of generations in his eyes. Now I knew the nasty business of being a cornered rat. It made no difference to that look that it was an accident with no malice on my part. I had erred in the late evening snow. My car had slipped purposely into his rear end. He would demand justice now, of that I was sure. I was the epitome of all the Black incidents in the city that caused him generations of discontent.

'But the street's slippery, I didn't mean to hit you.' I spoke hesitatingly, hating myself for being so mealy-mouthed, but knowing, against my will, that everything right now depended on that Cadillac man.

'Do you have insurance?' the Cadillac man asked.

'Stand up like a man!' exploded inside of me.

The Cadillac man spoke again. 'I asked you, do you carry any insurance?'

'Yes ... yes ... with Allstate.'

'Well, now, so do I.' The hostile look vanished. 'Show me your card. We can trade info and be on our way.'

'Hey, stand up, White man! Are you going to let that Niggra get away with that?' an angry voice shouted from the crowd.

A tenseness clouded the face of the Cadillac man. Slowly he turned in the direction from which the voice came. His hand, in a sweeping motion, jerked off his checkered English-style cap, and he violently flung it to the snow-covered pavement.

'Why don't you crawl back into your hole? He and I can settle this. We don't need any more of your shit.' Then he turned to me. 'Don't you think we can settle it?'

'You're right, we can!' I responded with a quaver in my voice. Inside I felt I had to answer that voice too.

'We don't need your two cents. All of you.' I waved my arm boldly around at the crowd and sneered. 'Just leave, we can do it ourselves.' The crowd seemed stunned for a moment, then slowly began to disappear.

'Let that Niggra-lover settle his own. He's probably got Niggra blood in him anyway.' A parting shot from the disappointed fading crowd.

As I turned back to the Cadillac man, our eyes made contact for a moment of recognition before I added, 'Now, as you said, let's exchange insurance information and be on our way.'

A MARK OF DIGNITY

A murmur of voices piqued our curiosity as my wife and I walked slowly down the church aisle for a last view of her aunt. We simply could not understand the cause for this undertone. Such a disturbance at a funeral was down right sinful. We quickened our steps to see what the problem was.

The woman lying in state was no saint. At one time she was the belle of Chicago. She loved her liquid refreshment and gala hoopla. I first met her when I made a stop in Chicago on my way home on furlough from the Navy. I had been recently married, and my new wife and I where going to spend a few days with my parents. We had to change trains in Chicago, so we thought we would see some of the windy city before making our connection.

My wife made contact with her aunt, and the time spent with her was full of lighthearted merriment. She fascinated me with her indomitable spirit and lust for life. She was a classy lady. Each time we went out, she wore a stylish hat. When complimented about her choice, she simply laughed and said, 'My symbol of royalty.'

Finally, we said our good-byes and headed for the train station. But as we boarded, I heard a voice calling my name. It was this wonderful woman. In her hand she carried my navy coat which I had left at her house. I really appreciated her thoughtfulness then, as I did on several other occasions through the years.

Near the end of her life, she came to stay briefly with us. Whenever she accompanied my wife and me on a rare jaunt somewhere, whether it was hot or cold outside, she always left the house with a modest hat of some kind, a symbol of her elegance. On one occasion when she couldn't find her hat and my wife said she could go without it, she calmly emphasized each word as she said, 'My hat exhibits good breeding, a respectable upbringing.'

As we moved up the aisle at the funeral, the whispers around the coffin became more audible. 'I don't think that is at all appropriate,' one person remarked. 'But she does look natural with it,' another commented. 'The idea of burying a person like that!' a third person observed. 'I just can't believe it!'

We hurried forward to see what they were jabbering about. To our surprise, in the coffin lay my wife's aunt with a hat crowning her head like a tiara.

We stood silent for a few minutes. Then, my wife whispered, "Her hat is so characteristic of her. I think it's a good touch, don't you agree?'

Looking down at her, I couldn't recall a time that I saw her out of the house without a hat. It seemed from the time she put it on until she returned home, she always wore her sign of gentility. I nodded to my wife in agreement.

We took a seat in a pew and waited for the service to begin. The coffin was closed and draped with the burial cloth. The pastor of the church stepped forward and bowed his head in prayer. Then, he put his hand on the coffin and stood for a long moment looking at the people assembled.

At last, he spoke, 'Many of us have mixed emotions about burying this good lady with her hat on. I listened to the various comments trying to find out where I stood on the matter.' He paused and looked around the church.

Out of the corner of my eye, I saw many heads bobbing in agreement. A low buzz accompanied these gestures.

'I thought of all the reasons why this should not be done,' he continued. 'But the one overriding factor for me was that she wore a hat all her life — a meaningful symbol to her of the way she was raised. All her life, this was her style. And it showed not only style but class. More than class, it represented a definite dignity in the way she lived her life. I have no reservation with her being buried with her hat. Nor should you.'

He paused before he finished, 'After all, as she lived in life, so should she be honored in death. Should she not go to meet her maker wearing that symbol of style, class and dignity?'

Again with accompanying murmurs, the heads bobbed in agreement.

Later that morning as they lowered the coffin into the ground, I envisioned the lady with her precious hat. I knew that, wherever she was, she would have liked what the priest said about her and her hat. She would have liked his words about style and class.

But, most of all, she loved her mark of dignity.

Note 2 - EXTENDED FAMILY, THE NEW AMERICAN STYLE

For most people, 'extended family' means aunts, uncles, cousins, grandparents — that is, 'blood' relatives.

But the American-style of slavery made sure that Africans forcibly brought to America had no family — that is, nobody to speak the family language; no traditional family customs or clothing styles; no traditional religions. No husband could 'protect' his wife. No parent could protect a child. A parent could be sold at any time, as could any child. A slave could not 'jump the broom' with anyone without the master's permission.

Because the mothers were forced to work long hours, the children who were young enough to need 'day care' usually had no parent close at hand. Usually, an old woman who could no longer work in the fields (or wherever) would be in charge of the children in the slave quarters. Thus, 'family' became whoever happened to be in the quarters. In one sense, a child was raised by everyone collectively (the new 'extended family') because the slave-system ensured that traditional families could not exist.

Thus, in response to a specific evil of the slave-system, something potentially wonderful — the extended family, the new American style — was created. As a result, 'family' for many people now means anyone who is family 'in fact' . . . even if not 'in blood'.

JAMES R. BROWN

One of the first African American Chief Engineering Officers in the (civilian) Military Sealift Command, James R. Brown spent much of his off-duty time aboard ship writing stories for his children back home in Minneapolis Minnesota. Once he retired and was permanently ashore back in the Twin Cities, a major theme of his stories became growing up in the Twin Cities during the '30s and '40s. That theme is also present in *THE BARBERSHOP*, his 1995 play set in St. Paul.

THE DANCE GROUP

In 1938 I learned to dance. For a couple of years my family stayed with my uncle's family. They owned and ran the Harlem Club, one of the largest nightclubs in Spokane, Washington. With the help of our older cousins, my sisters and I were taught what was called Swing Dancing. It was the big band era, the time of the Jitterbug and the Lindy Hop, and I learned all the major steps. When my family moved back to Minnesota in 1940, I continued my interest in dancing. So, when I entered Minneapolis' Roosevelt High School in 1943, I started a dance group.

Because I was the only black male in my high school, I never dated. But once when my small group decided to go to a dance at the Marigold Ballroom, the five guys drew from a hat the names of five of the best girl dancers in the group to see who was to escort whom. I drew the name of a girl who had recently moved to the city from North Carolina. Her name was Elaine. She was a short girl with freckles, long red hair and a petite figure. Elaine was not especially good looking, but had a great personality and the quick, rhythmic moves of a natural dancer. She was popular, and the whole group was fascinated with her slow, southern-belle way of talking.

The night of the dance was a gloomy one. It had rained all day, that cold, late fall, Minnesota rain. My group used three cars that night, and we all followed each other to pick up the girls. Elaine was the last on the list to be picked up. I had chewed my fingernails to the quick; argued with my father until he let me use his 1936, blue Hudson Terraplane; and gone down to Keefer's Clothing Store and bought a new, white-on-white wing-collared shirt to wear under the warm-up jacket that went with my slightly pegged denim pants.

When we pulled up in front of Elaine's house, she was waiting under an umbrella on the front steps. She wore dark slacks, white bobby socks, black patent leather shoes and an oversized wool jacket of maroon and gold, our school colors. When she started down the walk toward the cars, I got out to greet her.

'Hi, Elaine,' I said. 'You look great!'

She gave me a half smile but didn't say anything. Her face was pasty white. Her eyes were red, and I hoped it was from the rain and not because I was the one who had drawn her name.

As I walked her to the car, the front door of the house flew open and a short man with a pot belly stumbled down the steps, hollering and cursing. His hair was disheveled, and fresh blood was splattered on the front of his dirty white shirt. He was barefoot and reeked of stale booze. He ran up to us and grabbed Elaine by the arm. 'You get your ass back in the house.' he said. 'If you think I'm going to let you go out of this house with a goddamn nigger, you must be crazy.'

Every muscle in my body tensed. Elaine's eyes glossed over, and freckles appeared on her reddened face. The other kids stared at us from the cars. Donald Petersen, one of the guys from my group, got out of his car and came up and stood by me.

'Papa,' Elaine said, 'go back to the house. Don't do this to me.'

Her father swung around and slapped her hard across the face. 'I told you to get your ass back in the house!' he shouted. 'Go in there and take care of your momma.' But Elaine stood her ground. She had dropped her umbrella and her hands cupped her injured face as the rain turned flame-red hair to dark coral. 'And you, nigger,' he slurred, coming right up in my face, 'you got less than one minute to get your black ass off my property.'

I stood there in the rain, fists clenched, teeth clamped tight in my jaw. The backs of my calves were trembling with fury. I wanted to fight. I wanted my knuckles to feel the crunch of nose cartilage. I wanted to stomp that puffy, flushed face into the ground with the heels of my shoes. But I did nothing. I just stood there steaming, hoping and praying he wouldn't be stupid enough lay a hand on me.

'Hey! Take it easy, mister.' It was Donald. He had hold of my arm. 'We just come by to pick up Elaine to go a school party.'

Then Elaine's mother appeared in the doorway, wobbled down the walk and put her arms around Elaine's shoulders. The mother's face was badly bruised, and blood ran from her cut lip. 'Come on now, John,' she said to her husband. 'I got Elaine and we're going back in the house.'

The drunken man turned toward his wife and Elaine, who was crying uncontrollably, and roughly pushed them back toward the house. 'You think I'm going to let my daughter grow up to be as much of a slut as you are?' he shouted at his wife.

By that time the other kids had piled out of the cars and gathered around. I knew they were there. I could feel their presence, but it took every ounce of self control to keep from going after the little, red-neck bastard.

My friends were coaxing me back toward the cars when Elaine's father returned to the front door holding a shotgun. Elaine and her mother were wrestling with him, screaming and pleading for him to put the gun down. But the father fought them off and continued hollering and cursing.

His abuse shifted from me to the group. 'You punks! You whores! You nigger-lovers!' My friends flushed. They averted their eyes from each other. None of them uttered a word. Donald got me back to my car and motioned for me to follow them.

My friends' cars pulled away from Elaine's house, and I, alone in the blue Hudson, followed. The temperature had dropped, the rain picked up, and I drove as if I were a zombie. My whole body was one big knot. I could feel acrid tears being wrung from my heart. Not the wet, clear tears dropping from the eyes like the morning dew drips from a lonely leaf, but those searing, bloody tears that ooze silently from a bruised organ. Those tears of hatred more than anger. God! How I wished I could have turned them off. At first they felt like a few burning drops, and then a trickle, like hot lava overflowing a volcano. The flow burned deeper inside the coils of my gut until the pain absorbed the hatred, and left only the anger, stored neatly inside.

I was brought up with the fallacy that to be a man one should not cry outwardly. No matter what or how great the hurt, a man should never show his tears. Man, the bastion of human strength, the thoroughbred of the species could never show weakness, and tears were the direct product of weakness, I knew it was all bullshit, because suppressed anger could only be maintained so long, and I'd often wondered how long before my volcano would erupt. But not that night. I was safe and in the perfect place: alone in the blue Hudson, in the dead gloom of a stormy night.

Somehow I'd lost track of my group. I sat in the car, the motor running, as the red ball of the stoplight glistened through the rain-splattered windshield. The blackness of night surrounded me. I was suffocating in its gloom but had no will or desire to break out. The Hudson was like a discarded coffin, thrown out on some barren dump site. Almost unnoticed, the red ball turned green. The rain splattered relentlessly on the metal lid, but I could not move.

The rap on the window did not startle me, nor did the flashing lights from the squad car behind have any effect. I couldn't move. My body was lifeless except for the torrents of burning tears being pumped from the ventricle of my heart. The car door opened, and cold, damp air invaded my coffin. I heard a gruff voice flowing through a hollow tunnel. 'What's the problem here, fellow? Let me see your driver's license.' But I could only shake my head. I wanted to be left alone.

My father came down to the police station. It was the worst night of my life. After that incident, things changed. I stayed in school, played football, did all the normal things, but nothing was the same. I never did see Elaine again. She dropped out of Roosevelt, and I heard she was going to a vocational school downtown. I met other classmates and continued my dance class during my remaining school years, but none of us were what you could call, friends. We were merely acquaintances.

I felt I didn't belong in that school or with those people. I felt as if I just didn't belong.

> *I was an outcast from the society of my peers,*
> *and an outlaw in the land of my birth.*
>
> *'I am a stranger with thee, and a sojourner*
> *as all my fathers were.'*
>
> Frederick Douglass

ALEXIS BROOKS DE VITA

Alexis Brooks De Vita, a native of Los Angeles, California, is completing her doctoral dissertation at the University of Colorado, Boulder. Her dissertation is the interpretation of the mythical and historical symbols in Pan-African women's literature (in English, French, Italian and Spanish). Her short story 'Safari' is essentially autobiographical. She writes that, 'In addition to my husband and four children, my belief system, writing and education establish the worth and purpose of my life — a spiral that seeks to understand and fulfill itself as it reflects and merges with larger worlds.'

SAFARI

My mother's back-to-Africa movement took us to Uganda just as Idi Amin Dada prepared a revolution.

My body and heart also were in revolution. So I began my first journal and kept it locked. My mother taught sciences at a teacher-training college. My brother went to East African schools. They seemed content to be in the motherland. I tried to be content.

I went to a Catholic school for a few months. But my first friend, Margaret, went home during the dreaded season of female circumcisions and never returned. I finished that school year at a wooden desk in my shuttered room, studying correspondence courses and imbibing Uganda's lush green through my bedroom window as I studied and daydreamed.

My mother's house sat in a compound near a back road. Dancing young college men preparing for circumcision came down that road, stamping and jingling bells strapped to their calves and ankles. Idi Amin's soldiers drove the road in jeeps. They took professors from the college in the night, the keening wail of new widows following on the cool air behind them.

I lifted my head from my books and drawings only for market, dinner, walks to the college library, and storms.

The sky would sink into grey and the earth rise like a pregnant belly to take in the pink cracks of lightning. The cracks seared upward and downward, sending women and children screaming at each other into their huts. I would go to my rusted-screen windows to feel the shutters shake with the thunder. Chickens strutted and pecked at the snakes that had surfaced, afraid of drowning.

I also loved the library and strolled to it down the red-pebbled path that ran in front of my mother's house. This space was my share of Africa, where the sun slid through thick cypress and mango trees to heat the dark braids that fell on my back.

Inside, the library was cool and dark green, and rank with the mold of warped books. I hid in there between the crackly sheaves that were my perfect lovers. The world inside me grew to embrace the words that conquered colonists had left behind. I read European classics and found my journals explained in them. The African world around me and the literary world inside me mirrored each other's hopes, each other's wars, dreads and desires. I trembled at the thought that I might find myself to be a creature full of desires.

But my green cocoon was soon sliced open and discarded.

The librarian told my mother that I needed socializing. And my mother came straight home and confronted me in our kitchen, between the pantry, where bananas, tinned goods, and the pungent local liquor were stored, and the kerosene stove.

'I'm sending you to boarding school,' she said. 'But first, would you like to come with me on a camera safari? Or go with some of the college girls to their village for the term break?'

To the village? Where Margaret had disappeared? I neither knew nor cared what 'going on safari' meant. But I was very aware that pubescent girls, exactly my age, were married and bearing babies in the villages.

And hadn't my mother already received two marriage proposals for me? She was angry about them, and I felt guilty and indecent about them. (Not that I would miss her, if I married. We had never liked each other.) I just wasn't ready to leap into adult life and expatriation. This reversing of the Middle Passage was a complicated business.

Who knew if my mother would fetch me back or simply demand a large bride price, if someone wanted to keep me in a village?

I chose the safari — which turned out to be my debut into an adult world that would demand all my capacity for feeling.

The safari actually began with the sighting of giraffe running against the dawn that spilled pale pink as far as the eye could see. The herd was ranged in by white-capped mountains and flocked by top-heavy thorn trees, their food.

Had the tour jeep startled them? Or were they a mirror of my own new ecstasy? For the night before I had sampled something of myself that was new and vast and indescribable.

Our tour group had slept in a Cistercian monastery. The friars, silent with eyes downcast, rustled in dark dominos over the stone flags they had laid with their own hands. They sat across from us at dinner and served us wildebeest they'd shot, skinned and cooked, with wine made from grapes they'd nursed from the arid northern Uganda soil.

An older monk did all the speaking for his brothers. He carried on a cultivated multilingual conversation while instructing a younger monk to rise from the brothers' bench and fill the tourists' glasses.

The young monk kept his wide brown eyes on mine as he brought his decanter. As he approached, something in his look or movements flooded me with my first sense of sexual shame. I had to look away from him. My eyes went no further than his pale sandaled feet.

It seemed to me that he stood very close as he took an infinity to pour. The dark red liquid curled upward from the bottom of my delicately straining glass, and the older monk said to my mother, 'Your daughter is very beautiful.' The monks murmured in Italian.

We slept that night on stiff white linen in narrow clean cells. The bright moon shone through the bars of my window. I cried myself to sleep, an old habit.

But this cry was special. The young monk had witnessed the loss of my molar as I bled and caught the tooth in a drinking fountain between the guest rooms. He came forward out of the shadows, asking my mother if he might help. She patted my back and explained, 'It's just a tooth.'

He had laughed and gone away. Laughed. At my distress? At the discovery that I was merely a womanly child?

Laughed.

The next day, we visited the Karamajong, a wandering tribe now fixed in their stony wasteland and, due to Idi Amin's relocation schemes, targeted for invasion by southern Ugandans. They had been drought-starved for two years.

A young mother in a beaded leather apron, her gums bare, gave me her large-eyed child to hold. She said things about him that I could not understand. We each spoke several languages, but none in common. She took my arm and showed me her empty millet-storage basket.

Grinning stupidly in the face of the woman's misery, I felt needed and helpless. I had nothing to give her and rebuked myself with her disappointment.

Sometimes people reach for each other across cultural barriers, and their fingers slip.

But on safari, I began to suspect that life might yet become luxuriant. Fireflies, torch flames and feelings burned in the night and lit the way through darkness.

An enormous African guide, two rifles and cartridge belts slung across his back, drove us nearly to Treetops, a hotel built in the trees above a watering hole. We got out of his van and walked under thick fronds of sunlit leaves, listening to the trill of bright birds and the chit-chattering of monkeys and baboons, through an actual jungle.

I had changed. I now wore elephant-hair bracelets and leather Masa'i wrist-cuffs with my tinsel-wrapped bangles. I wore Pakistani sandals cut from slabs of tires with leather rings to hold the big toe and instep. Rain and sweat evaporated from my feet, and laughter rose from my throat like steam.

I loved walking through the jungle.

But the guide shushed me. My noise might make elephants charge and, if they did, he would be the target because he would be shooting.

So I hushed for his sake. For myself, I could think of worse deaths than one pillowed in green and monkey calls.

There is no malice in the charge of an elephant. I did not know then that they were killed for my bracelets.

We climbed a ladder to a woven hotel like a giant reed-basket, hung with crystal chandeliers and set with lace tablecloths and napkins. After we washed and dressed, we were shown to the balcony.

We took tea with the local baboons. Mothers held their nursing babies and were on their best behavior, knowing themselves welcome. Waiters chuckled and chided in Kiswahili, tossing the single-parent baboon families chunks of pineapple.

I left the tourists to draw close to the baboons, who sat on their haunches and looked out with me into the lively jungle. It was here that I first felt at home in the world.

I sat up all that night at the small round window in my mother's room. Soft light fell below onto the watering hole.

Workers had spread a salt lick, and the animals came to lick and lap all night. As if in shifts, first came herds and clusters of gentle vegetarians, looking warily about before spreading or curling their swift legs, leaving themselves briefly vulnerable. Next came the innocent vicious. The fanged carnivores lounged long after they had refreshed themselves, keeping others away.

At the start of another pink dawn, I watched a lone rhino wander away and let myself drift to sleep. How did he get here, so far from the savannah? I wondered as I slept.

The huge man who drove us in a Land Rover to the savannah was sharp with the other tourists. I spoke Kiswahili with him, sparingly and rarely. He was gentle with me.

One day, as we roasted in the Rover, I leaned towards the driver's seat with a rehearsed request. He listened and said nothing.

But at sight of the next perfectly-picked zebra skeleton, he swerved the Rover to a stop. Tourists gasped but said nothing as I stepped down from the Rover and approached the ravaged zebra.

Breathing deeply, I walked slowly under the high hot sky. This was my chance. This was my test.

I walked the border of my womanhood and faced life that ends. A strong brave hunter waited behind me. But I was alone, entering the life that leads to death and is grateful for the moment.

I gathered the sunbleached halves of a jawbone in my hands from the dust where my ancestors had risen and lain again. So this was my motherland.

Back in the Rover, I smiled at the driver. He smiled back at me, the only time I ever saw him smile.

Note 3 - ONE WOMAN AMONG MANY

Harriet Tubman is justifiably famous as a conductor on the Underground Railroad for leading several hundred fugitive slaves to freedom (without losing one to bounty hunters).

To help in the passage to freedom, a well as to convey other surreptitious messages, women (slave and free) developed a 'language of the quilts' to convey information to other African Americans. For example, hanging a quilt outside the door meant that the dwelling was a 'safe house' for food and rest.

Harriet Tubman also served the Union army during the Civil War as a scout and a spy. (Other black women, who were able to move freely as servants among southern white men, proved to be effective spies too.) Harriet Tubman's wartime service was so effective that she was awarded a federal pension by a special act of Congress. However, this award was not approved until 1897 (32 years after the war). And then it was reduced from $25 to $20 per month because of the bitter opposition of southern congressmen.

RICHARD F. GILLUM

An award-winning poet, Dr. Richard F. Gillum is a physician and biomedical researcher who has published over 150 articles on cardiovascular disease and related topics. The grandson of a former slave who became a Methodist District Superintendent in Kansas, he, his wife Brenda and their daughter, Faith Marie, live in Silver Spring, Maryland. Author of the books of poetry *I DON'T FEEL NO WAYS TIRED* (1984) and *NOTES FROM AN UPSTAIRS ROOM* (1994), he won the Seaton Awards for poetry from *KANSAS QUARTERLY* in both 1983 and 1986.

MOVING DAY

'Frank! Frank! You gone to sleep in that shed? I want us to get to Emporia before dark.'

'I'm comin', Jenny. I don't want to be leavin' nothin' I might need in town,' Frank replied with irritation.

He led their milk cow out of the shed and tied her to the back of the wagon. He seemed to have shrunk inside his faded overalls, and his gait lacked its usual crisp quickness. His nut brown face was drawn as he adjusted the furniture, rolls of bedding, boxes of pots and pans, and their remaining supplies. As he jerked on the ropes holding the load, he gazed over the wagon at the fields with their brown autumn stubble. He thought back to June of 1879 when he had first set eyes on this homestead.

Fresh out of the Ninth Cavalry he had ridden up the Santa Fe Trail from New Mexico to find a home in the Free State of Kansas. A white preacher in Council Grove had told him of the homestead colony of blacks founded by old Pap Singleton at Dunlap. He had heard neither of Singleton, who had been helping blacks from Tennessee move to Kansas for years, nor of the frenzied exodus of blacks from Louisiana, Mississippi and Texas who fled white bulldozing and starvation wages in the spring of '79.

When he arrived at Dunlap, he found families camping in the open, in makeshift tents or under wagons. At first it seemed a colorful scene. Women in long homespun dresses tending the fires or carrying water from the river, small children sleeping on quilts on the ground, or running among the women. Then he realized many families had neither teams, plows, supplies, nor money to buy them. Most of the men were off looking for work at nearby farms.

Good land sold for six dollars an acre. He had been lucky arriving with his horse, and nearly $200 in an old sock in his pocket. Within days he had scouted out this homestead, set up camp, bought a harness and plow and set to work getting in a crop of corn. The crop did well and besides tending it he was able to scythe enough prairie grass for a winter's worth of hay. He put up a one-room shack and a lean-to for the horse and bought a few chickens.

The winter of '79-'80 was mild. He found time from his work to ride around and meet his neighbors. That was how he met Jenny. She had come west with her sister and brother-in-law from Davidson County, Tennessee. Jenny had two children, Dinah and Buddy, by a man who had run off and left her. Given the dearth of eligible women, the prospect of a ready-made family did not deter Frank from calling on her steadily through the winter and marrying her in the spring of '80.

The next six seasons had been good ones by dent of hard work, and favorable land, weather and prices. Frank enlarged the house to four rooms as his family expanded by three.

Then the rains failed and crops were scanty. Farmers were hit hard and there was talk of a depression in the towns. Jenny had never liked the harsh realities of homesteading. Although she worked hard on their farm, she regularly let Frank know that she thought they would be better off in town where, in addition to his earnings, she could be paid by whites for the nursing and midwife services she often rendered free or for a few bartered goods to their indigent farm neighbors. She also wanted schooling for the children.

While times were good, Frank put her off with talk of improvements to the house and a few months of part-time school in Dunlap for Dinah and Buddy. But after the second crop failure, he could resist no longer. He rode to Emporia to find work.

After three weeks he had the promise of a job as a gardener and houseboy for a well-to-do white family, an offer for his farm at two dollars an acre, and he found an affordable house to rent.

The last yellow leaves of the cottonwoods along the Neosho were falling as he rode back up the river with the good news. Frank's initial flush of excitement at his unexpected success in town had left him by the time he had covered the nearly twenty miles to the homestead. He took care of his horse before going slowly to the house to give Jenny the news. When the children's excited greetings and queries about candy and presents subsided he stated in a matter of fact way, 'Found a job in town and a place to move to. I can get something for the farm too.'

'That's wonderful,' Jenny beamed, 'isn't it children? We can live in a town with stores, and a school, and streets, and a church.' She hugged each of the children and then turned to Frank. 'You don't seem happy about the good news,' she said, noting his limp response and emotionless face.

'Oh, I'm happy all right. It'll be fine for you and the kids.'

'I suppose you'd rather stay on this damn farm and starve.'

'I never said that. I said I'm happy. We'll leave in a couple of days and you'll never have to set eyes on this place again. That's what you want, ain't it? So just let me be.'

He snatched up his hat and stalked out of the house. He headed by habit for the fields.

Frank said little at supper or the next day as they boxed the little store of goods accumulated over the past eight years. It didn't seem like much to show for the back-aching, brow-sweating toil. But the land was his, his to farm in any way he pleased. If only the rains had returned this year. Maybe he could have hung on to his dream of building the place up, expanding even when Buddy and little Joshua grew old enough to work at his side. Then he would have something fine to pass on to them and their children. But no, it couldn't be.

'You gonna stand there gazin' off into space all mornin'?' Jenny snapped, impatient to be underway.

'Alright, alright. I'm just thinking of what I might be leavin'.'

He turned from the wagon and went back to the house for one final check. He looked fondly at the rough board walls and swept dirt floor, after hesitating a moment, he stepped inside.

Jenny had put the children in the wagon, and now as Frank lingered in the house, they wanted down again. After forbidding them to move, she stalked to the door, hands on hips, to ferret Frank out and get him going. Looking in the door she saw him standing in the center of the room, head down shoulders shaking. She approached slowly, wondering if he was sick. As she reached his side she saw he was crying.

Aware of her presence, he said huskily, 'I'm going to miss this old place.'

Jenny stood still not knowing what to say.

As if coming to himself, Frank wiped his face brusquely on his sleeve, put his arm around her shoulders and hurried her towards the door.

THE TELEGRAM

Sergeant Joseph Williams cursed under his breath as he rounded the barracks. Dust rose in angry puffs beneath his boots. The screen door creaked irritably as he entered, stalked past the bunks to his cramped alcove. Disgusted, he threw his hat on the bed and then cursed all the more as he snatched it away again, fearing even more bad luck.

'I knew it had to come, but why now? June 7, 1918,' he muttered, reading again from the orders in his hand. He glanced at the calendar tacked to the wall. Today was Thursday, May 30. 'A week from tomorrow then.' Returning his eyes to the paper, he read again.

'The 317th Sanitary Train will entrain for duty with the A.E.F. in France at 7:30 am, June 7, 1918, from Camp Funston, Kansas.' Skipping down the page,' ... expected arrival at Brest on or about June 25, 1918.'

His mother, his sister Ruby, and his girl Edith were to arrive from St. Louis on the eighth. Women visitors were allowed at camp only on the first Saturday of the month. Now it seemed that he would be on a belching troop train the other side of Chicago before they came.

'Damn this white man's army, this white man's war' He sat down hard on the lumpy bunk and with a kick sent his hat skimming across the floor.

'Why did they have to draft me anyway? I could care less if the Kaiser kicks Frenchy's butt or vice versa. It sure ain't worth dying or getting gassed or crippled over.'

Soon he heard the bantering rumble of the other men returning from the mess hall. The sound filled the barracks, little impeded by the flimsy partitions of his room. Some of the men would stay in the barracks until lights out, lounging on their bunks, talking in small groups, playing cards or dice. Others would leave for the colored 'Y' hut to see the moving picture or to pick up at few things at the canteen. Those who could read and write might buy paper and stamps for a letter home or peruse the newspapers or magazines. The sergeant was frequently among the latter. Despite dropping out of school after the ninth grade, he could read and write well, often reading or penning letters for the other men. But tonight he would stay put.

He swung his polished black boots up onto the bed and lay back with his hands beneath his head. Staring at the peeling white paint on the ceiling, he tried to keep his mind off the guns and gas and trenches of France and on his womenfolk. He was by no means the only man in the 317th expecting visitors the day after their departure. There must be a way to have one last visit or at least a glimpse of them. At the very least they should be spared the expense and disappointment of a fruitless trip to Camp Funston. If letters went out in the morning, they would scarcely arrive before the women departed. There would be no leave granted before entraining. Telephones or telegrams would be fast enough. But neither the men nor their families at home had access to telephones — only top brass had that in the army. Even the men who had money for telegrams would probably not be able to get to Manhattan, the nearest town, to send them off. Passes would be nearly impossible to get now, especially for the colored troops. But if he could go on behalf of the men, send off their telegrams and return. Or if one of the officers could go. As much as he hated to, he would have to ask Lieutenant Wing for a favor.

He swung his feet to the floor, picked up his hat, dusted it against his pants and left the room. He hurried past the men, barely acknowledging their greetings with a wave of his hand. The sun was slipping beneath the horizon as he walked through the shadows. He hoped to find the lieutenant at the HQ offices, knowing he would receive a distinctly unfriendly reception at officers' quarters. Luckily, the lieutenant was there, sitting at a desk, doubtless working on preparations for his unit's departure. The sergeant stopped at the open door and knocked on the jamb. The lieutenant looked up and frowned when he saw who it was.

'What do you want at this hour, Williams?'

'Sir,' said the sergeant, saluting and standing at attention. 'I have a request to make on behalf of the men.'

'Well, make it fast. I'm busy.'

'Yes, sir. Well, a lot of the men were expecting lady visitors from out of town on Saturday the 8th of June. These men need to get messages to their womenfolk not to come, since we're leaving on the 7th. The regular mail will be too slow for men a long way from home. If you would grant me a pass for Saturday afternoon, I could take all their messages to the telegraph office in Manhattan and save the women and men a lot of worry and disappointment.'

'I suppose you have a woman coming the 8th?'

'Yes sir, I do. My mother, sister, and a friend.'

'I thought so. Or maybe there's some gal at the YWCA hostess house that you're itching to get at another time, or one at one of the houses.'

'No, sir. I just . . .'

'Save it, Williams. I haven't the time. There will be no more passes before entrainment. With some real action in sight, some of you boys might never come back. That's all. Dismissed.'

The sergeant saluted, turned crisply and disappeared from the doorway. He left the building with clenched fists, muttering, 'Damn him. What did I expect from that cracker lieutenant? I better not hear of any white soldiers leaving on the seventh getting passes.'

He laughed bitterly. 'Or what? What am I going to do about it? Sure, they'll get passes just like they get the best barracks, uniforms, food, gear, and everything else.'

He was glad he hadn't spoken to the men about his idea. Many of them had left for the 'Y' hut when he returned. He tried to hide his anger and disappointment as he stretched out on his bunk again after undressing.

His mind circled the problem like a wolf circles a wounded but dangerous stag. He could go to the captain. But he could expect less from him than from the lieutenant. He could slip off the base. No, too risky. If he'd wanted prison, he could have refused the draft. The problem seemed to give no opening for an attack. He got up, switched off the light and lay in the dark. He listened to the men returning from the 'Y' hut. The moving picture must have ended. The joking and talking continued until lights out. Then the barracks became quiet, save for scattered snores and coughs.

Crickets chorused outside the window, and the sergeant's mind slid down the sound toward sleep. He saw a boy playing with Brownie, his chocolate colored spaniel with the white breast. He heard his mother calling. Must be suppertime. The boy went in the house and found his mother crying beside a coffin in the parlor. Was it his father? There was a flag on it. Maybe it was . . .

A soldier's bout of coughing followed by, 'Shut up, Harris. Turn over or somthin', man,' dragged him back from sleep. For a moment he felt warm and happy as he thought of Brownie and his mother. But then there was the coffin and, now fully awake, he remembered the problem. Neither Brownie nor his mother could help with that. The women . . .

Suddenly he remembered some of the men talking about a white Travelers Aid Society worker in Manhattan who had gone out of her way to help their women visitors get settled when they arrived for a visit when the men were tied up in camp. Maybe she could help now. In the morning he would send her a letter — it should arrive in a day or two. He'd include the names and addresses of expected visitors and the money for the telegrams. He frowned to think how easy it would be for this strange white woman to simply pocket the money and throw away the letter. After all, these men would never return to Funston.

He shook off the thought. He would compose the letter now, get up early and get the information from the men and mail the letter on the way to mess. He was mulling over the fifth version of the text when he finished his slide into sleep.

It was August when his mother's letter reached him at Raon l'Etape in the St. Die Sector. They were manning the field hospital for the 365th Infantry out of Camp Grant. Near the end of the letter, he read a line that made him pause and smile: 'Oh, and thank you, son, for your telegram that saved us a long trip out to that camp for nothing.'

YOU NEVER WOKE ME

'I say we do it, daddamit!'

Sam jabbed the tines of his pitchfork deep into the stable floor and left the sweat-darkened handle vibrating the air as he stalked out of the stall.

'I say we do it now, tonight!'

'Aw Sam, there you go gettin' crazy jes cause I say give the old man a little more time.'

'He's had all the time I'm givin' him. Black folks supposed to be free near seven years now. These 'prenticeships we're in ain't supposed to last forever. Jes until we're grown men and know our trade. I'm grown. Been grown. And so are you. We've learned all we can learn on this farm about ridin', and drivin', and trainin', and feedin' horses. And we sure know all about cleanin' stalls. This 'prenticeship is just a white man's trick to get out of payin' us the wages we should have been gettin' for the last year or more. Waitin' don't do no good . Beggin' don't do no good . I'm gonna take my back pay and ride west on it.'

Sam walked past his brother and into the next stall to stroke the back and shoulder of a big chestnut gelding. At the familiar touch, the horse turned to look at Sam, trailing hay from the manger, then returned to eating.

'That's right, Brownie, you an' me gonna make tracks out of here.'

'But Sam, they'll say it's horse stealin' and when they catch us we'll go to prison sure if the KKK don't lynch us first.'

'If you take that black mare yonder they ain't gonna catch us.'

'I don't know, Sam. I'm scared. Even if we give the sheriff and the Klan the slip, do you know the way from Kentucky to this Kansas you keep talkin' 'bout. I don't know, Sam. I say we wait a while longer.'

'Go on an' wait 'til you're an old gray-headed stable boy with nothin' more than you got now. I'm goin' tonight and I'll find Kansas or somewhere better than here. You think about it real hard. After dark I'm goin' to slip over to Barker's farm and say good-bye to Jenny. I'll be back at our cabin by midnight. Get some sleep if you can. I'll wake you then and we'll ride out together or else we'll say good-bye.'

Sam left his brother to finish the evening stable chores. Back at their cabin, he tied his few belongings in a shirt along with some cornbread he had managed to wheedle out of the cook at the farm house.

Crickets were chorusing in the deepening dusk as he slipped out of the cabin to cut through the tobacco field to the road. Jenny and her mother would probably be asleep by the time he reached the Barker place. The moon was new but its glimmer would be all he needed to negotiate the familiar fields.

He had only been on the road a few minutes when he heard the hooves of perhaps a dozen horses on the road behind him. Turning he saw the glimmer of lanterns. A black apprentice was not supposed to leave the farm without a note from his master. Sam instinctively slipped into the bushes by the roadside and crouched waiting to see who would pass. A stabbing pain started in his stomach and worked its way up towards his heart as he listened to the rough voices, often raised in laughter, grow nearer, The knife in his belly turned when he glimpsed the white robes in the lantern light and caught snatches of conversation.

'Yes sir, that's one nigger that'll never vote Republican again, much less talk some others into it . . . '

'Hey Bob, did you see his eyes roll when we put the rope 'round his neck.'

'Yea! Bet he'll hang there three days 'fore the other niggers have nerve to cut him down.'

The gang, now square in front of Sam, let out a roar of mirth. Sam thought the knife had transfixed his heart and that he must keel over in the thicket and be dragged out to be the next swinging corpse of the evening. But he did not fall and the hoofbeats, and shouts, and laughter passed on up the road and out of hearing. Sam opened his eyes and saw only an empty country road.

Next morning his brother shook him angrily.

'What you doin' still here! I was ready to go at midnight but you never woke me.'

HISTORICAL NOTE: Although the preceding story is fictional, oral accounts indicate that two black brothers from Kentucky did indeed arrive on horseback in Kansas at about the period of the story, one of them being the author's maternal grandfather.

Note 4 - 'LEARNING WOULD SPOIL THE BEST NIGGER'

The education of Frederick Douglass was motivated, in part, by his master in Maryland ordering his new wife to stop teaching the young slave to read because it was 'not only unlawful but unsafe.' The master also said, 'Learning would spoil the best nigger in the world. . . . It would forever unfit him to be a slave.' Years later, Douglass wrote, 'In learning to read, I owe almost as much to the bitter opposition of my master, as to the kindly aid of my mistress.'

In Kentucky, Mila Granson ran a 'midnight school' to teach reading and writing to other slaves in the area, twelve students at a time from about eleven in the evening till two in the morning. When those twelve learned the basics, twelve others took their places, until several hundred had 'graduated'. Among them, a number wrote their own passes to get a start on the underground railroad to freedom.

Within five years after the Civil War, over 4,300 schools serving over 250,000 children born into slavery were started, with many adults going to the schools in the evening after the workday was done.

HAZEL CLAYTON HARRISON

The founder-president of her own technical writing, training and consulting firm in Los Angeles, California, Hazel Clayton Harrison is also a poet and short story writer. The mother of two, she is the former president of the Los Angles chapter of the International Black Writers and Artists. First introduced to Africa (Zimbabwe and Nigeria) in 1993, she visited South Africa the following year. Then in 1996, she returned to South Africa with her husband Terry and her son Elias. She co-authored (with Ginny Knight) the book of poetry *A MOST DEFIANT ACT* (1985) and wrote a book of stories and poems *WINTER IN L.A.* (1992).

AN EXPERIENCE IN COLOR

I will never forget the first time my family went from Ohio back to Georgia on vacation. It was the summer of 1956. My father had bought his first car and wanted to show it to his family. So he loaded all six of us in it and drove home.

The South was filled with images, colors, and sensations that are forever ingrained in memory. There was the horror I felt while watching my father wring a chicken's neck, and then watching it run around the yard with its bloody head hanging from its body. There was the wonder I felt as I looked at hills of red dirt and clay. There was a feeling of disdain for the big, old hogs that greedily ate the slop we tried to feed the hungry little pigs. There was the sense of being better than my southern cousins because they used outhouses and had never seen snow or ridden on an escalator. There was the wonderful feeling of freedom as I ran barefoot through fields. There was the sweet taste of watermelon and fresh cut sugarcane.

At first the sounds of our laughter and play filled the air, but after a week Willie grew tired of feeding the chickens and hogs and playing in the yard. Mother tried, in vain, to find things for him to do. Finally, she threw her hands up and said, 'Boy, I don't know what I'm gonna do with you. Here take this quarter and take your sister to the movie.'

Willie strode ahead of me, kicking sand and dust as we followed the narrow road into town. The sun stood directly over our heads when we reached the theater. It was just opening. While Willie bought tickets, I lingered at the popcorn stand wishing I had a nickel. When I looked up, he was walking toward me. 'Come on,' he said, motioning for me to follow him. I followed him toward the darkened movie. We were just about to go inside when, in a southern drawl, the usher shouted, 'Hey, the Colored section is upstairs.'

I turned around and looked up at him. I was trying to figure out what he meant. What colored section? Was it a special section that was painted in different colors?

I did not know what it was until we were sitting in the balcony. Looking down, I could see only whites seated on the main floor. We were the only Negroes in the whole theater, and we were being forced to sit in the Colored Section! I felt as if I had suddenly developed a contagious disease.

I had heard of segregation before. I had heard that in some places Negroes were forced to sit in the backs of buses and to use separate toilets, but I never reasoned that I was to be among those to be segregated. All my life I had gone to school with whites and sat next to them in movies. So why was I being separated from them now? Unable to formulate an answer to my question, I squirmed in my seat. I glanced over at Willie. He was slouched far down in his seat.

I was staring blindly at the screen when I realized I had to use the bathroom. I waited a minute before telling Willie, hoping that I could hold it. When I could wait no longer, I leaned over and whispered the awful news to him.

Feeling a terrible sense of dread, I followed him down to the lobby. The urge to urinate intensified when we found no sign of a restroom there. Finally, in desperation Willie went up to the usher and asked him where it was. A puzzled look crossed the usher's face as he leaned back against the wall and said, 'Why, there ain't no restrooms for Colored folks around here, boy.'

I fought the tears that welled up in my eyes as I followed Willie back outside. I wondered what Negroes who lived in town did under these circumstances.

Outside, we avoided looking into each other's eyes. The sun felt hotter than ever. But there was nothing left to do but go home. We headed home in silence, too ashamed to talk about what had happened.

When we reached the dirt road, Willie turned his back while I went behind a bush to pee.

THE PASSING

As I sat in the waiting room at St. John's hospital, a feeling of helplessness washed over me. My mother was dying and I was totally unprepared. She was still young — only fifty — and still so beautiful. I looked at the picture my father had given me a few hours earlier. She smiled at me; teeth bright, flashing; eyes dark and wide; hair thick and black. I looked closer. Did I see myself in her? Everyone said I looked like her. Now she was dying and there was nothing I could do.

'Let's go get some coffee.' My sister Delores' strained voice interrupted my thoughts. The past few days had been like climbing a rugged mountain, but somehow the pressure of death had brought us closer together.

'Sure,' I said, 'let's go.' I squeezed my father's shoulder and told him we were going downstairs. God, the pain in his eyes. Had I ever seen it so deep? I asked him if he wanted a cup of coffee. He nodded his head and again assumed that distant look like he was remembering, remembering a time when they were together.

In silence, we took the elevator downstairs. The hospital was quiet, bare, white. The sound of squeaking nurses' shoes scratched the air.

We paid for our coffee and sat down at a table. I hadn't seen Delores since she left for Nigeria a year earlier. She had flown in yesterday, but instead of spending the night talking as we normally would have done, we had spent all our time at the hospital sitting in the lounge and moving zombie-like between the lounge and the intensive care unit where our mother lay hooked to a respirator.

'So how you been Dee?' I broke the silence that submerged us. She looked up from the cup she had been staring into as if there were tea leaves at the bottom she could read.

'OK, I guess,' she half-smiled like it hurt the corners of her mouth. 'Still adjusting to Nigeria, but other than that, I'm OK.'

I looked deeper into her eyes, trying to read into her words. I knew my sister. If something was bothering her, she wouldn't say it, but you could read it in her eyes.

'How is Victor doing?' I changed the subject. Everything we could talk about seemed so depressing. I was tired of depressing subjects.

'He's fine, just fine. When we got your telegram, he wanted to come too, but we couldn't afford another plane fare. He was so upset. He loves Momma too, you know, almost like his own mother.' There was a catch in her voice.

'I know,' I said. 'Everyone loves her.' It is true. Everyone who knows her loves her. She has a beauty that comes from some inner source. It is a strength, I guess. God, why do you have to take her?

Silence engulfed us again. We were both thinking of her lying in that barren room, hooked to that damned machine. When I touched her, her hand was cold, limp, heavy — totally unlike the hand I knew; the one that tenderly bathed me, combed my hair, dressed me, and spanked me when I got out of line.

The doctors said it could be minutes, hours, or days. She had had a massive cerebral hemorrhage. Even if she lived, they said, she would be a vegetable.

'What do you think we should do, have the respirator turned off?' Delores' question mirrored my thoughts. I sighed and took a sip of coffee. It was a question we had all asked ourselves. The doctors had laid the burden of the decision in our hands.

'It's the most painful decision we'll ever have to make, Dee. But we've got to make it.' I was picturing that damned machine, breathing its harsh air into her lungs. I was thinking of the thin lines of blood that trickled from her mouth. I was thinking of the pain in my father's eyes. I was thinking of the waiting — waiting for her to die.

'I can't stand to see her hooked to that thing,' I blurted. 'She wouldn't want this. I know she wouldn't want to linger. She should be able to die in peace.' I tasted the salt of my tears, a taste that had become so familiar.

Delores studied her cup again. 'Yeah, I guess you're right,' she said softly.

There was silence again. The cafeteria was empty except for a cashier who was busily wiping a counter. It was eleven o' clock. Time to go back upstairs and wait. I reached over and squeezed Delores' hand. 'Come on, let's go back upstairs.' I gave her a reassuring smile and we walked together toward the elevator.

When I asked my 83 year old great Aunt Lily whether we should have the respirator turned off, she shook her head and said she did not know. But she added that in the old days when someone was dying, the family removed the pillow from beneath their head to make it easier for them to pass from this life. I took this to mean it was OK for us to have the doctors turn the respirator off.

Mother died on Friday, the day we were to meet with Reverend Harris, who was to help make the awful decision. She died quietly at dawn, almost as if to protest the decision we had to make — a decision that God had, after all, already made.

The day of the funeral dawned cold, wet, and gray. I awoke feeling that if I could make it through the day, I would be alright. I felt like today was the culmination of a long, terrifying nightmare — a nightmare that would leave me forever changed.

Trying to be careful not to awaken my eight month old nephew who was sleeping, peacefully cradled, next to me, I slipped out of bed and tiptoed over to the dresser. The face that looked out of the mirror at me was a hopeless mess. Dark rings circled my eyes. A mess of hair sprung from my head like barbed wire. Did I look as old as I felt? I pulled a pick through the barbed wire, then decided that it didn't matter how I looked. I was, after all, in mourning.

It was seven o' clock. The house was full of people — aunts, uncles, cousins, from New York, Boston, Atlanta, Miami had arrived by train, bus, car, and plane. It seemed ironic that they should all come after her death. Why didn't they come when she was living? But something told me that they had come to comfort the living as well as to mourn the dead.

I pulled on my mother's old flannel robe and crept downstairs, stepping over huddled, blanketed forms as I made my way through the living room. My relatives would be rising soon and I felt obligated at least, to have a pot of hot coffee ready for them when they awoke. Besides, messing around in the kitchen made me feel useful and gave me a chance to be alone with my thoughts and prepare for an ancient ritual I had been able to avoid until now.

The funeral was to take place at one o' clock at Quinn A.M.E., the church my mother had belonged to since she had come to Steubenville when she was barely eighteen years old.

After sitting in the kitchen sipping coffee and making small talk with my aunt, I went back upstairs. I knew there would be a long line waiting for the one bathroom in the house, and I wanted to get a head start.

There was flurry of suitcases opening and closing, a rustling of slips, dresses, suits, and the gurgle of water running in and out of the sink as we dressed. The confusion was heightened by rushed patter of footsteps in the hall, the voices of incoming neighbors and friends, the heavy sighs of my father who could not decide what tie to wear, and the cries of my nephew who didn't want to be shoved into his brown, corduroy jumper.

By noon when the funeral director arrived, we were all standing downstairs waiting. A tall, thin, man with wire rimmed spectacles, Mr. Smith looked like a funeral director. After a prayer was said, he began directing us into a line. Then holding an umbrella over my father's bowed head and slumped shoulders, he led us out to the limousine.

In silence, we rode the five blocks to the church. How many times had I been a spectator in this parade? How many times had I watched a stream of black limousines cruise by carrying the grieving family? Now I was in the parade. It seemed strange, like being in a play and in the audience at the same time.

The church stood like a small brick fortress on the corner of Fourth and Washington Streets. The last time I had entered it was with my mother over a year ago. Her eyes had shone that day when she introduced me to her new pastor.

Inside the pews were filled with familiar faces. Single file, we marched past row after row of faces that loomed out of my childhood. Even the faces in the choir were ones that had been there when I was a child. It felt like I was in a time machine or in one of those old black and white movies.

In front of the church before the altar, my mother's body lay. It was a shadow of her former self. Her white gloved hands lay folded across her chest. Her eyes were sealed shut.

I felt the eyes of the congregation on me as I moved slowly toward the casket. Were they expecting me to break down and weep as I had seen Jewish women do at the wailing wall of Jerusalem? I hated to disappoint them, but I felt no rage, no anger, no urge to throw myself on the casket. Not even tears would come.

I stopped momentarily before her body, searching for some expression of my grief. Finally, I reached out and touched her hand. I mouthed the words, 'Mother, I love you,' hoping that somewhere, somehow, she would hear.

Note 5 - 'PATTEROLLERS WAS DE DEVIL'S OWN HOSSES'

The slave system in the U.S. efficiently kept poor whites (most of whom would have been peasants or members of the working-class in Europe) from forming alliances with black slaves. The poor whites needed work, and the slaves had too much work, including virtually all of the skilled jobs (such as carpentry, blacksmithing, masonry, etc.).

Thus, one on the major types of work available to poor white men was to help the slave masters 'keep the niggers in their place' — that is, help preserve the slave system that made sure poor whites had no proper employment themselves. This employment usually took the form of armed patrols on horseback at night to terrorize slaves who were away from their owner's property. (In a sense, these patrols were the forerunner of the Ku Klux Klan that was formed right after the end of the Civil War.)

These armed patrols were so necessary as part of the control system that the 1852 Code of Alabama, Section 983, stated: 'All white male owners of slaves . . . and all other free white persons, between the ages of eighteen and forty five years, . . . are subject to patrol duty.'

The terrible cruelty inflicted by these armed patrols on any slave caught without a proper pass obviously impressed people. For example, most slave-church gatherings kept two or three men on watch in case the patrollers ('patterollers' or 'paddyrollers') showed up.

Most regions had a slave song that carried variations of these sentiments:
'Run, nigger, run, de patteroller git you,
Run, nigger, run, de patteroller come;
Watch, nigger, watch, de patteroller trick you;
Watch, nigger, watch, he got a big gun.'

As one former slave said years later, 'Patterollers was de Devil's own hosses.'

LEON KNIGHT

The 'white grandfather in a family of color — the color is black', Minneapolis writer Leon Knight says that he is disappointed to find it necessary to still specify such things in the United States of America. His book of short stories, *VERA'S RETURN* (3rd printing, 1995), has been used in English courses at two colleges. His latest book is *IF, BECAUSE OF ME memories and love poems for Ginny* (1996). Because of their family, he and Ginny, his mate for over 40 years, have seen things very few others are privileged to see. Thus, he also says, 'From where I stand, I find life to be fascinating. I wouldn't have missed it for anything.'

A STRANGE AND SIMPLE STORY

I want to tell you a story told to me by a woman who wouldn't have told me unless she believed it was true. The story shows that sometimes life is more strange than we believe it to be . . . and often more simple.

* * * * *

Some years before the Civil War, a German immigrant settled on a Kentucky farm near the Ohio River. He and his wife were newly married and planned on having a big family to work the farm, as people did in those days. But after having a daughter named Maria, something happened so they couldn't have any more kids.

Still, the German was a top farmer, and his wife Eileen worked right along with him in the fields, as Maria toddled along after them. But, with just Eileen and him doing the work, he knew that they could work only so much land . . . even after Maria got old enough to do her share.

Then during fall harvest, they saw a wagon coming down the road. A farmer they didn't know was passing through with his family. The German and his wife told the strangers that they could pull their wagon onto their place and share some food before moving on the next morning. And that's what they did.

As they shared a meal in the fading light, it became clear that the stranger wasn't much of a farmer, even if he did have two slaves to help him do the work. The stranger also complained about his 'good-for-nothing' slaves. The 'buck' was passable, but the 'nigger-bitch' was worthless and always wasting time with her sick brat. But the German could see that the woman's main problems were that she had been overworked, abused and underfed. He could also tell that it bothered Eileen to see how the slave-woman had been treated.

When the German said that maybe the woman, like any good stock, just needed better care, the stranger got mad and told him, 'Who said she's good stock? And if you feel that way, why don't you buy her?'

The German had never considered owning slaves, and he knew his wife was strongly opposed. But when he looked at Eileen, she softly said, 'As long as it includes the child.'

The German and the stranger haggled about the price well into the night but, since the stranger was so cash-poor, the German finally got a good price.

The next day, everything was made legal at the courthouse.

So that's how Sarah and her little boy Joshua became the property of Wilhelm and Eileen Schneider.

And the German was right about the slave-woman. Under Eileen's direction and with proper food and daily fresh milk, Sarah and Joshua were both almost fully healthy by early winter. They were also able to move into the tiny cabin the German rough-built back under the trees.

In the spring the fieldwork went much faster with three grown-up workers. Sarah even took over most of the chores with the animals. So the German was able to spend longer hours in the fields while Eileen went in to fix supper and Sarah milked the cows. Meanwhile, Maria and Joshua followed after whichever grown-up interested them the most.

That year, for the first time, the farm really prospered. But when the German went into town, he heard some mean talk about how he had his wife working right along with a slave. When he told Eileen about the gossip, she said, 'It's our farm, and I like to work ... like it better than going to town.'

So after that, she didn't go into town very often. She and Sarah would even sometimes spend time together when they didn't have to. And their children grew up together on the farm — Eileen's daughter and Sarah's son ... Maria and Joshua.

When the children were about seven or eight, they were already working on the farm ... though Maria did spend a few months each winter going to school. But she didn't like it much, except that she did enjoy teaching Joshua his A-B-C's. By the time she was twelve, she was done with school, and she and Joshua also were pretty much doing grown-up work. By the time they were fifteen, there was no farm in the township that could top the Schneider Farm.

Of course, up to this point, there's nothing strange about this story — I'm just coming to that....

When she was about seventeen, it was getting time for Maria to consider marriage. But that would mean she would have to move away from the farm, and nobody wanted that. So the German didn't mention it for awhile.

But when she passed eighteen, the German couldn't delay the matter any longer and told her that it was time to get married. She agreed readily and, without hesitation, said, 'I want to marry Joshua.'

'Joshua?' he said in amazement. 'You know a white girl can't marry a slave.'

'But I could marry him if he was free. It can be your wedding gift, and then Joshua and I could stay here on the farm. We've talked about it often ... being here on the farm together forever.'

When the German shook his head in wonder and looked at his wife, Eileen just said, 'Wilhelm, don't you have eyes to see anything?'

'So it's all right with you?' he asked.

'Of course,' she replied.

When they talked to Joshua, he agreed readily, though he did have one request — 'Does Mama go free too?'

About a month later, manumission papers were filed at the courthouse freeing Sarah and Joshua Schneider. In the fall after the crops were in, the

German crossed the Ohio River with Maria and Joshua so the two young people could be married as Joshua and Maria Snyder by an abolitionist minister.

And that's the story about how a white girl married her daddy's slave... a strange story, indeed.

* * * * *

But what's so 'simple' about this 'strange' story?

Well, what could be more simple than a young couple getting married and eventually taking over the prosperous family farm?

INCIDENT AT THE MALL

I want to tell you a story, son, from before you were born. I'm telling you now not only 'cause I'm your father and you are old enough to hear it but I think you've got sense enough to see the truth in what I'm talking about. At least, I hope you do. No, make that... I *pray* you do.

* * * * *

I was young... though some older than you — yeah, I remember... I was 21, about half done with my bachelors degree. And I drove out to the mall where your future mama worked... you know, just to say 'hi' and to let her know I'd be picking her up later.

As I walked through the mall, I heard this ruckus and went over to the small crowd gathering. There I saw two cops — one white and one black — rousting three boys, all black.

The black cop had two boys pretty well under control... so they were out of it. And the white cop had one boy with his hands up on the wall and was yelling at him to 'spread 'em'. Then he kicked the inside of the boy's leg... you know, down on the ankle bone. And this was before high-top shoes got so popular.

Anyway, the boy's leg flew up, but when it came down, the cop would yell and kick him again. After this happened a couple of times, a woman in the crowd called out that the cop didn't have to be so mean to the boy. When some of the other people agreed, the cop kicked the boy again... especially hard this time. And then still using his hand to grab the boy's shirt and push him against the wall, he turned around to stare at the woman who yelled.

So I walked a bit closer and looked at his badge number to write it down in my little notebook. When he saw that, he let go of the boy and walked over to push his chest into my face. 'Take a good look, boy.'

I moved back slightly so I could see his badge more clearly, checked his number against what I had written, and said, 'Thank you, Sir.' When I stepped back into the crowd, two women, including the first one who yelled — I think they were Puerto Rican — came over to tell me I had done the right thing.

Meanwhile, the cops had sent the three boys on their way, and the crowd was beginning to disperse. So I went on about my business.

But a few minutes later when I was coming out of the shop where your mama worked, I saw the two cops . . . one on either side . . . obviously looking for somebody. I suspected it was me, so I slipped back into the shop where I could watch them a bit.

When I saw the two Puerto Rican women going by, I went out and walked along behind them. Just as we got close to the black cop, I passed them.

Sure enough, the cop wanted to 'talk' to me. Lucky for me, the two women stopped again to watch. But when (in a generally hostile way) the cop checked my identification, one of the women asked him what he was up to.

And when he said, 'Stay out of this, lady,' she said, 'We know what you're doing and why you're doing it. And we're prepared to be witnesses.' Her friend didn't look like she was so sure about that.

But that didn't matter 'cause the cop backed off. But before he left, he leaned over and growled in my ear, 'You may have my partner's number, but we know your name and where you live.'

By that time, the other cop had joined him. And the two of them walked away a bit to stand whispering together and glaring at the three of us.

To say thanks, I treated the women to some coffee at one of the stands. The lead lady insisted on giving me their names and telephone numbers . . . 'just in case.' And I was grateful that they did.

Later as I approached the main exit to the mall, I noticed a cop car waiting in the 'no parking' zone right in front . . . my two 'friends' again. So I stepped back to wait and watch.

About fifteen minutes later, when they hadn't moved, I checked the nearest telephone directory and called the local police precinct. It took some time to get through to the watch commander, but I finally made it.

He was irritated but officially respectful when I told him my story, including the fact that I had the names and phone numbers of two witnesses. He wanted to know why I was telling him this over the phone, rather than filing a written complaint.

'I don't want to be pulled over a couple of blocks from the mall on a minor traffic offense and have the hell beaten out of me for resisting arrest.'

After he protested that his officers would never do anything like that, I asked why I could still see them outside the mall from where I was phoning. He assured me that they must have other reasons for being there. So I told him, 'Good. Then, since all of your calls are recorded and I have my witnesses, neither of us has anything to worry about.'

After I hung up the phone, I stayed in the booth where I could see the squad car. Within two minutes, it drove rapidly away from the 'no loading' zone.

I waited about a half hour before going out to my car. After I started the motor but before I drove out of the lot . . . just in case somebody was waiting for me down the road, I eased open the secret compartment I had specially built in the panel of the door to get quick access to my gun.

But, as you now know, I didn't have to use it that day. Since I've grown older, I've learned how foolish it is to be carrying a gun.

* * * * *

Well, there it is, boy, one of the many stories I could tell you about how I almost didn't live long enough to become a daddy to you.

THE THREE OF US

Mrs. Louise Wilcox moved slowly about her kitchen, as she always did in the morning before her bones loosened up, but more quietly than usual because her granddaughter MariLou, who was still sleeping, didn't get to stay overnight very often.

She quietly hummed as she mixed the batter for pancakes — having someone to cook for again, even for a day, was a good feeling. Thirty-five years as a cook, first at the daycare center and then at the school, were not something a person could forget easily. And Daniel — God rest his soul — loved eating. He would lean back in his chair after breakfast, pat his stomach and say, 'Oh, Lou. Those pancakes were so heavy that I won't be able to cross any bridges till sundown.' He would say the same thing every morning, and she loved it every time.

When she heard water running in the bathroom, she turned the burner on under the skillet. A couple of minutes later, her granddaughter, dressed in a loose, sleeveless nightgown, came in from the bedroom. 'Morning, Grandma.'

'Mornin', baby. You want some eggs with your 'cakes and sausages?'

'Oh, Grandma,' MariLou said as she hugged her grandmother from behind, 'you'll get me fat — the way you fed me last night and everything.'

'Fat? You're 14 and skinny as a pole. With all the energy you burn off — what with dancin' lessons and tennis lessons and everything you're in at school — you don't have to worry about gettin' fat. At least, not yet.'

'Do you think I'm too skinny, Grandma?'

'You're not too skinny — and you're not too fat. You're just right — healthy and you've got good bones. And you never did answer — do you want eggs or don't you?'

'Yeah. I'll have two — over medium.' The girl pulled her nightgown tight around her and looked over her shoulder. 'Grandma, do you think I'm getting any figure yet?'

Mrs. Wilcox looked lovingly at her granddaughter for a long moment. 'Sure. You're gettin' some — I mean, that's not just baby fat. You've got a trim little body. I'm sure you'll be a beauty when you grow up.'

'Oh, you're my Grandma. You'll think I look good, even when I weigh a ton.'

Mrs. Wilcox poured another cup of coffee as MariLou started her breakfast. 'Your grandfather loved his breakfast. Seems like I haven't fixed 'cakes since he passed.'

MariLou laughed. 'You fix me pancakes everytime I stay over, or when you come out to our place.'

'And I said 'it seems like' . . . Do you know what I mean by that, baby?'

MariLou nodded. 'I think so . . . I was thinking about Grandpa Dan last night. In bed there beside you — wondering what it must be like. Did you live here when Mama and Uncle George were small?'

'Yeah. Ever since your grandfather and I got married — in 1946, just after the War. Oh, that man was handsome in his uniform. He was a member of 'The Red Ball Express.' That's where he learned his drivin'. So he always had a good payin' job. That and bein' a veteran, we were able to get this house. We were just about the first to buy around here — the neighborhood was just changin' over then.'

The girl seemed puzzled. 'Changing over?'

Mrs. Wilcox nodded, pleased with being able to teach her grandchild. 'This area was all white — mostly Jewish. Some were willin' to sell to Negroes . . .'

'Negroes? Oh, Grandma, don't you mean "blacks"?'

'Don't interrupt your grandmother. And Negro is a perfectly good word. I can remember a time when nobody wanted to be called "black" — it was almost as bad as bein' called "nigger." '

'Is that right? I didn't know that.'

'Baby. There are lots of things I want you to know, but I can't tell you how glad I am that there are some things you don't have to know.'

They were silent for a minute before MariLou asked, 'Grandma, are you coming to my dance recital on Sunday afternoon?'

'I sure am, baby. Your mama's comin' to get me early in the mornin'. Your recital is one of the few things I'm willin' to miss church for.'

'But won't you be attending service with us?'

'Oh, yeah — of course. But I meant missin' my own church.' She looked at MariLou for a time before continuing: 'The idea — my grandbaby studyin' ballet. And with the best teacher in the whole Twin Cities. At least, that's what your mama says.'

MariLou smiled shyly before breaking into a wide grin. 'Grandma, I'm the only black girl on the A-Team.'

'A-Team?' Mrs. Wilcox asked, pleased with her granddaughter's pleasure.

'The recital is divided into three acts — Beginners, B-Team and A-Team. It won't say that in the program, but that's what it is. And I'm on the A-Team.'

'Imagine that. My grandbaby dancin' ballet — on the A-Team.'

'Actually, it's "modern" ballet.' The girl jumped to her feet, put her arms up in the classic ballet pose and did a couple of steps. 'It has the ballet steps and movements, but with modern choreography.'

'Ballet steps, but with modern chor-e-og-raphy.' The old woman glowed with pride. 'Oh, my, aren't you gettin' to be somethin'?' She held her arms out to the girl, who 'danced' over to ease herself on to her grandmother's lap.

'Do you think I'm getting too big for this, Grandma?' MariLou asked as she nestled her head into the woman's shoulder.

'You'll never be too big for this. At least, I hope not.'

'Yeah.' The girl snuggled contentedly against her grandmother's breast. Then she asked, 'Grandma, what would you say if I told you I had a boyfriend?'

'Well, you're gettin' to that age. So it wouldn't surprise me at all. Why? Do you have one?'

'No. But I'm thinking about it.' She sat up and looked at her grandmother. 'But what would you "think" about it?'

'I think your mother didn't raise a fool. None of the rest of us did either. So, when you think you've met the right boy and you think you're old enough to handle it — I think you'd do just fine. I know a lot of girls your age 'go crazy' with their boyfriends. But I don't think you would. In fact, I've been kind of surprised that you didn't have a boyfriend by this time.'

'Oh, Mama freaks out whenever I even mention 'boy.' Whenever she sees an article about teenage pregnancy — especially if it mentions black and unwed mothers — she'll put it out on the kitchen table for me to read. I get so tired of statistics. I try to tell her, 'Mama, I'm not a statistic.' And she says, 'I don't want you becoming one.' It really makes me fed-up some times.'

'I know, baby. But your mama is just doin' the best she can. You know, it's hard raisin' kids these days.'

'Do I know? Oh, tell me about it. But, Grandma, at the senior high, they have a special program for the girls with babies. And those are white girls.'

They were interrupted by a sound on the porch. Mrs. Wilcox eased MariLou off her lap and was half way to the window before a knock sounded on the door. Mrs. Wilcox peeked cautiously around the curtain. 'Oh, it's just Freddie.' She turned back to MariLou. 'You go put a robe on, or wait in there till he's gone. We'll finish our talk later.'

Mrs. Wilcox raised the shade over the window in the door before removing the chain and opening the locks. 'Good mornin', Freddie. Come in.'

'Morning, Mrs. Wilcox. I found your hammer. The Johnson kid had it.' The young man, about 18, placed the tool on the kitchen table.

'You mean, Lionel?'

'No. The little one — Damian.'

'Damian? Why he's no more than 8-years-old. Why would he steal my hammer?'

'He just saw it on your back porch and decided he wanted it. You got to be careful what you leave out, Mrs. Wilcox.'

'I usually am, but I got careless this time. Thanks, Freddie.'

'No problem, Mrs. Wilcox. And Damian won't bother you no more. Lionel and me told him not to mess around your place again.'

He brightened up as MariLou, wrapped in her long robe, came in. Mrs. Wilcox said, 'Freddie, this is my 'granddaughter.' MariLou, this is Freddie.'

'Well, good morning to you, 'granddaughter' of Mrs. Wilcox.'

MariLou blushed and said, 'Hi.'

'Freddie,' Mrs. Wilcox asked, 'will you be goin' by the library?'

'For you, the 'grandmother' of MariLou, I can go most anywhere. What do you need, Mrs. Wilcox?'

'I have a couple of books to return.'

'My pleasure, It will be no trouble at all.'

As Mrs. Wilcox got the books from the living room, Freddie said to MariLou, 'I play drums for 'Spontaneous Combustion.' Ever hear of us?'

MariLou shook her head.

'We're kinda big in the area. Come and hear us sometime, and I'll introduce you around.'

'Okay,' MariLou said softly.

'Here are the books, Freddie,' Mrs. Wilcox said as she returned to the kitchen. 'You're sure it's no bother.'

'No bother at all,' Freddie said. 'Well, I better be shufflin' off.' And, for MariLou's benefit, he did a Michael Jackson 'moon walk' to the door, spun around once and was gone.

MariLou looked at her grandmother and started giggling. 'Grandma, who is that boy?'

'Evidently a boy who likes you,' Mrs. Wilcox teased.

'Where does he go to school?'

'He dropped out a couple of years ago. He's mentioned joinin' the navy, if he can't get a decent job pretty soon.'

MariLou frowned. 'Oh, darn. A drop-out.' She flicked her hand through the air. 'Well, so much for Freddie.'

'What do you mean by that.'

MariLou sighed. 'I don't have time to be interested in a 'drop-out.' Any boy for me has to plan on going to college — at least.' Suddenly she stiffened and cocked her head to listen. 'Mama's coming.'

Mrs. Wilcox looked at the clock. 'Your mama already?'

'Yeah. I can tell the sound of her car.'

Then Mrs. Wilcox heard it too — the high-pitched sound of the diesel-engine as a car pulled to a stop in front of the house. A few seconds later, the rapid 'clack-clack' of high-heeled shoes sounded on the sidewalk leading to the kitchen porch. Mrs. Wilcox opened the door before her daughter could knock. 'Good mornin', Brenda. You're a bit early, aren't you?'

'Morning, Mama. I was feeling 'antsy' so I left as soon as I could.' She looked at MariLou. 'Girl, who was that I saw coming out of the house?'

'It was just a boy, Mama.'

'I know it was a boy. But what boy?'

'That was Freddie,' Mrs. Wilcox said. 'He came by to see me — to take some books back to the library for me.'

Brenda looked first at her mother and then at her daughter. 'Well, okay.' Then she held out her arms to hug her mother. 'Good morning, Mama.' Then she turned to MariLou. 'You too, girl.'

'Good morning, Mama,' MariLou said, returning the hug. 'I didn't know you'd be here so soon. I'll hurry and get my things packed.'

'No hurry, girl. I'm early and I need to talk to your grandmother anyway.'

Mrs. Wilcox poured her daughter a cup of coffee and got out the milk as MariLou headed for the bedroom. 'I don't have any nutra-sweet,' she said.

'Oh, sugar won't hurt me once in a while,' Brenda said. She sighed heavily as she poured the milk into the coffee.

'Didn't you have a good time at the banquet last night?' Mrs. Wilcox asked.

'Actually, it was a going-away party for someone who got promoted to the company headquarters in Houston. That went fine. But I really got bummed out at work yesterday.'

'Let me fix you some cakes as you tell me about it. The batter's right here.'

'Oh, no,' Brenda began, and then weakened. 'Well, okay. Just a couple.'

Mrs. Wilcox smiled as she whipped up the batter again and turned on the stove. 'Well, what happened?' she asked.

'I had to fire someone yesterday. I know it's part of my job. But I think I got used.'

'Why do you say that?'

'It was a young black woman. A single mother. Several men could have told her but, no, they tapped good-old-black-woman Brenda to be the hatchet man. She really told me off.'

'Told you off?' Mrs. Wilcox repeated.

'She called me a lot of names — including some I haven't heard in a long time. But what could I do, Mama? She missed too many days — was late the rest of the time — and didn't get her work done when she was there. She just wasn't working out. And other workers are willing to carry someone only so far.'

Mrs. Wilcox sat down again as she placed a plate of pancakes before her daughter. 'Those things happen, dear. As you said, it's part of your job. You'll feel better after you eat.'

'She said I didn't remember who I was or where I came from — that I didn't have any sympathy for anyone else who is trying to better herself. She said nothing has changed for 'real' people like herself except that it's now 'Oreos' like me — white niggers — who are standing on her head. She called me an 'Uncle Tom' — doing the white man's dirty work.'

'Oh, don't pay any attention to what someone like that says.'

'But, Mama, what if it's true?'

'It's not true. And she better not let me hear . . .'

Brenda interrupted. 'She called me an 'educated fool.' Mama, what if I am?'

'At least you're educated.'

In spite of herself, Brenda started laughing. 'Oh, Mama. What would I do without you? 'At least I'm educated.''

Mrs. Wilcox didn't share in the laughter. 'I'm not jokin' about this, Brenda. Fools like that really make me mad. A lot of people worked hard to clear the field and to break the first sod. And then some fool like that comes along who won't even till her own garden. She wants to blame 'Uncle Tom' when she goes hungry. It's people like that who are really betrayin' the dream. Not you. A lot of people struggled long — and some died — to open doors for us. And your daddy and I worked hard so your brother and you could have the chance to do things we never could do. So don't let a fool like that make you feel guilty.'

Brenda smiled shyly at her mother and nodded. 'I don't know why I was ever so lucky to have such a wise woman for my mama. You're right, of course — just like you always are.' She leaned back in her chair. 'I knew I had good reason to come early.' Then she leaned forward again. 'Mama, why don't you come out to live with us? That area on the 'walk-out' level can easily make a nice little apartment for you. I know MariLou would love it. And I really worry about you staying much longer in this neighborhood.'

Mrs. Wilcox shook her head. 'How many times do I have to say it — this is my home. I'm just two blocks from church — and they really need me when they have church dinners and functions. Besides, I have my work at the daycare center.'

'That's just volunteer work — you can do the same at a daycare near us.'

'This is a 'special needs' center. Henrietta Hawkins' daughter Evelyn runs it. Some of those babies need an old woman like me to just hold them because they get abused at home.'

'But the news reports say that the county takes babies out of homes like that now.'

'Well, Evelyn reports a lot of abuse that the county does nothin' about. So I try to help her out as best I can. I need to be here to go hug those babies. I may be in my sixties and retired, but I can still be of some use.'

'Yeah, I know. But, sometimes I need you too — like today. And sometimes I do need help with MariLou.'

Mrs. Wilcox extended her hand to pat her daughter's arm. 'No, you don't.'

Puzzled, Brenda looked at her mother. 'Mama?'

Mrs. Wilcox smiled gently. 'Sometimes you don't realize what a good job you've done raisin' that girl. You don't need any help at all.'

Brenda smiled her appreciation. 'I still would like you to come and live with us. When I think of all you and Daddy did for me, I want to do something for you now.'

'Well, there is one thing that you can do for me.'

'Anything. Just name it.'

'Let MariLou come to stay with me more often.'

When Brenda inhaled sharply, Mrs. Wilcox pressed on: 'I know you don't like her bein' in this neighborhood very much — and I'm glad she doesn't have to go to school here — but this is where you grew up. And she'd be with me all of the time.'

Brenda sighed, 'Oh, Mama.' Then she called, 'MariLou.'

MariLou's hair was half combed when she stuck her head into the kitchen. 'Mama?'

'Since there are just teachers' conferences at school today, how would you like to stay with your grandmother?'

The girl's eyes sparkled. 'Oh, can I, Mama?'

'I have a late meeting. So I'll pick you up about 6:45.'

'Thanks, Mama,' MariLou said, before disappearing back into the bathroom.

'Can you come for supper?' Mrs. Wilcox asked.

'No, but I will bring dessert, if that's all right? I'll phone John, and we can go out later to get something. But for early dessert, it's just the three of us. Okay?'

'That sounds fine — just the three of us.'

Note 6 - THE FIRST BLACK PILOT

Bessie Coleman, who was born in Atlanta, Texas, in 1893, became very interested in flying about the time of World War 1. However, because no one in the United States was willing to teach her, she had to go to France after the war and then learn the French language before receiving instruction. She earned her license from the Federation Aeronautique International in 1921, thus becoming the first black anywhere in the world to become certified as a pilot.

MILLER NEWMAN

Prof. Miller Newman teaches English at Montgomery College, Rockville, Maryland, and with her husband David Gadson, heads up an extended family, including her first grandchild, in Washington, DC. Her story 'Johnny Reb Was A Black Man' is an account (fictionalized, of course) of real events in the lives of some of her ancestors. She says, 'Most families have stories far more interesting and complex than history would generally have us believe. My job is to tell the stories of my family.'

JOHNNY REB WAS A BLACK MAN

When they came to tell Kelly Miller that he had been conscripted into the Confederate Army he was not surprised. The whole of Fairfield County, South Carolina, had been talking about the war. And after his brothers and their families had told him that his wife Elizabeth and the child she was carrying were free 'cause President Lincoln had signed the Emancipation Proclamation, he knew that it was just a matter of time before they came for him. And come for him they did.

Kelly Miller was a freeman — was born a free man — and had built up a solid reputation as a carpenter and farmer. That's how he had met Elizabeth. She was owned by Mr. Labon and worked on the plantation along side her daddy and two brothers. She was tall and strong, just like they were, and could work the farm and keep the house for her father and brothers just the same. By the time she was proclaimed free she was pregnant with their fifth child.

But when Major Souls began to organize the unit from Winnsboro nobody overlooked Kelly Miller. He did not go because he believed that black people should be slaves; his first four children and their mother were owned by Mr. Labon. And no matter how respected he was, he knew that his wife and children were vulnerable. So he went — 'conscripted' they said — to fight on the side of the South.

But this story is not about what happened during the war. It's about what happened long after the war was over. The child Elizabeth was carrying when she was freed was one of the only two of the Miller children who were educated. Kelly Miller, Jr. was sent to school after the war. He was only six-years-old, but he was one of the beneficiaries of the free public education that was offered to Negroes in the South.

He left Fairfield County when he was sixteen-years-old to attend Howard Preparatory School in Washington, D.C. A promising student in mathematics, Kelly Miller, Jr. completed the preparatory program at Howard and went on to graduate from the university department. As a graduation gift, he returned to Fairfield County and bought the 200-acre tract of land that his parents had been farming for shares for most of his life.

Kelly Miller, Jr. prospered in Washington, DC. As a member of the Howard

University faculty he became an activist and advocate of education for the Negro. Every summer he would leave his wife and children and travel throughout the country recruiting young Negroes to attend Howard University.

Often caught between the philosophies of two of his contemporaries, WEB Dubois and Booker T. Washington, Kelly Miller, Jr. was seen as the voice of reason between the two men. As the plight of the Negro worsened in America, Miller, a prolific writer and orator, was a vocal opponent to the injustices that he saw sweeping the nation. He seized whatever opportunities he could to draw attention to the plight of the Negro. His newspaper column 'Kelly Miller Speaks' was syndicated and appeared in over 100 newspapers.

But when his father, Kelly Miller, Sr., died, at the age of 97, he returned to Winnsboro to bury him. The story Kelly Miller, Jr. (Papa) told of the funeral goes like this.

A Confederate veteran who lived on the adjacent plantation came over to the house and asked permission to ride with Papa to the funeral. He stated that he and Kelly, Sr., the last survivors of the old regiment, were comrades, the same as the other soldiers. He asked if Papa would have any objection to his placing a Confederate flag on the coffin.

Papa explained, 'I was on the spot. How could I let my father be buried under a flag that stood for everything I had spent my entire life fighting against? I thought about it. But when I looked at this man who like my father had spent his entire life on South Carolina soil I knew that I had to put my own feelings aside. So, with great misgivings, I consented to his request.'

As the funeral procession passed the old soldier's house he alighted for a moment to go in and find the Confederate flag. He returned shortly with a Union flag instead, saying that he could not locate the stars and bars. He added, 'This is perhaps better since the stars and stripes now wave over us all.' Papa responded with a silent nod, and a loud inward 'Amen!'

So it happened that when Kelly Miller, Sr.'s coffin was taken from the hearse it was covered with the stars and stripes, placed there by the last veteran of the Winnsboro Unit of the Confederate Army.

READING DADDY'S WILL
(from *GOD DON'T LIKE UGLY*)

The day after Daddy was buried beside my mother in a Catholic cemetery, we gathered at home for the reading of the will. We were all in the living room except Martin, the youngest, who said that he didn't want to hear it and went into the kitchen to fix himself something to eat.

Jack, Jr. sat down and started to read. By the time he had finished the first page, Martin decided to join us and, plate in hand, announced that he was now ready to hear the will. 'Start over,' Martin said. 'I missed the first part.'

'Too bad. You said you didn't care what Daddy said.'

'Well, I'm here now,' he said, picking up a fork full of yellow egg yolk. 'And

I want to hear it from the beginning. What did he leave me?'

Lucy was livid. When she saw Jack actually going back to the first line, she bolted across the room. 'Don't you dare go back. If he was interested in what it said, he should have had his sorry ass in here.'

Martin looked up from his plate as he sopped up the last bits of his evening breakfast with a wedge of toast. 'Why don't you sit back down. Nobody was talking to you.'

'Well, I sure as hell am talking to you,' Lucy shouted.

I caught Sandra's eye and she rolled her eyes up into her head. Lucy stood threateningly over Martin.

Martin sneered, picking up another pony Miller's Lite. 'Get out of my face. I want to hear the will from the beginning. Go on, Jack.'

Lucy grabbed the now-empty plate from Martin's hand. 'Who the hell do you think you are? We are halfway done and you come in here demanding that we start over 'cause you were too triflin' to get your ass out here. The hell with you. If you want to know what it said in the beginning, then you can read it yourself when the official reading is over.'

She glared at him and went on. 'They did teach you to read before you dropped out of high school, didn't they? We are not going back. Every time somebody wants to get something done, you want to change it to suit yourself. We are not going back.'

I walked slowly over to Lucy and slipped the plate from her hand. She was so close to breaking it over Martin's head that I feared for his scalp.

'Lucy, calm down,' I said. 'Jack can go back. What difference does it make anyway.'

Jack Jr. began to read again — 'My twenty dollar gold piece I leave to my son William. And to my grandson Stephen, I leave my watch....' Daddy didn't have very much so the will was short.

It was not until Jack, Jr. got to the part that left the house and pretty much everything in it to me that Martin went into one of his performances. What it really said was that, if the house was ever to be sold, six of us had to agree but that Martin could have no say in the matter.

'Wait a minute,' Martin said. 'Read that part again.'

Jack Jr. reread the part that said in essence that Martin didn't have any say about anything.

The next ten minutes are a blur. Everything happened so fast. One minute we were sitting there listening to our father's Last Will and Testament, and then Martin was shouting, 'Damn y'all! Daddy didn't say that. You just want to cheat me out of what I should get.'

Furious and more than tired of Martin, Jack Jr. had Martin in some kind of headlock and was screaming at William to open the front door. When the door was finally open, Jack half dragged and half carried Martin out of the house. Martin, kicking and flailing his arms, went through the door screaming.

But summoning an adrenaline high, Jack, Jr. got him all the way out the door and onto the front stoop before Martin was able to halt the advance by bracing his feet against the brick knee-wall that surrounds the stoop. Martin used the wall to plant his feet and pushed back with all his drunken brute strength into Jack's chest.

Jack, Jr. did not release his hold, however. But the wall gave way and went crashing down into the basement entrance below. That did it. The neighbors came out to see what all the commotion was.

My cousin John picked up Martin's feet and helped Jack, Jr. carry Martin down to the sidewalk where they released him. Martin, more embarrassed than anything, vowed that he would get them when he came back. But he decided to accept defeat for the night and walked up the street, disappearing into the shadows, cursing everyone as he went.

'Go home, Martin,' John shouted into the night. 'Don't bring your ass back here again, unless you really want it kicked.'

My family began to disintegrate that night.

Note 7 - 'NO RIGHTS A WHITE MAN HAS TO RESPECT'

The Constitution of the United States requires agents of the federal government or of the government of a nonslave state to return any run-away slave to the slave owner (Article IV, Section 2).

However, when they could, many nonslave states simply ignored that provision of the constitution. (The 'return of property' argument was the primary claim before the court in the case involving Joseph Cinque and the other Africans who mutinied and took over the slave ship made famous in the movie *AMISTAD*.)

So, compromise between 'free' and 'slave' was always the name of the political game in congress, with those from slave states wanting 'more' as the nation expanded and those from nonslave states willing to accept 'no more'. This led to the Missouri Compromise of 1820, in which Missouri (slave) was added to the union along with Maine (nonslave) to retain the balance between slave and free states (12 each).

However, the Missouri Compromise also limited the expansion of slavery into most of the newly opened Louisiana Purchase. (This was only about a decade after Lewis and Clark returned from their famous exploration through the Northwest to the Pacific Ocean.)

On the other hand, the law confirmed the legality of capturing fugitive slaves in free states and territory. As a result, bounty hunters vigorously chased fugitive slaves into northern states, and slaves escaping with the help of the underground railroad often ended up in Canada to avoid their pursuers. Even Frederick Douglass himself went to England for a few years to escape the bounty hunters.

Dred Scott, the slave of a Missouri doctor who moved in 1837 to Illinois to serve four years as an army medical officer (and for a shorter time at Fort Snelling in what is now Minnesota), sued for his freedom when he was returned to Missouri as a slave. The case was in and out of courts for years until it was finally settled by the U.S. Supreme Court in 1857. In a judgment written by the Chief Justice Roger Brooke Taney (who was himself a slave owner), the court ruled (on a seven-to-two vote) that the 1820 law was unconstitutional because Congress did not have the authority to outlaw slavery in any state or territory and that an African American, free or slave, 'has no rights a white man has to respect.'

Thus the issue of 'Slave or Free' was 'settled' by the Supreme Court. Every state in the union and all of the territory of the United States would, after 1857, be slave. There could be no more 'compromise'.

GRANT WAYNE

A reclusive writer in Minnesota, Grant Wayne writes parables because they are short and simple and suit his somewhat cynical view of contemporary American life. But he also believes that 'parables, these simple stories that try deliberately to teach people about real life, have never succeeded in teaching very many people very much about anything. But I write them so I don't go crazy myself. At times, I know how Jeremiah felt.'

A WINNER THIS TIME — a parable
(The Bed-Box — $349.95)

The three men and two women in the crowded editing room watched the TV monitors intently.

Angelo, who would not say which side of fifty he was on, was the oldest of the group by far and also the most nervous — this may very well be his last chance to make it big. Ideas didn't come so easy any more. And he had come close a couple of times. He didn't want to get his hopes up too high too soon. But ..... maybe this time.

'It may be premature to be looking at this,' the long-haired man said. 'We haven't put in the music yet.'

'But I've got a real handle on that,' broke in the crop-haired woman. 'I really understand the concept . . . .'

'Well, let's see it,' Angelo said. 'I've been out hustled on a couple good ideas before 'cause it took too long to hit the market.'

Long-hair nodded, and the short guy with glasses pushed some buttons. A moment later, the main monitor screen went black. White letters slowly appeared — 'Over 17,000 Americans killed by gunshots each year.'

'We start with silence,' crop-hair announced.

The screen cut to black. Female voice-over: 'Are your children safe tonight'

The camera zooms back slowly, and the black becomes the funeral dress of a grieving mother.

'Dramatic here,' crop-hair went on. 'Starts thoughtful. Builds intensity.'

Zoom into the casket — angelic little girl. Female voice-over: 'Valerie was six . . . in her bedroom at night . . . a drive-by shooting . . . random violence in the neighborhood . . . killing our children.'

Close-up on the mother's tear-stained face — fade to black. Letters on the screen, with female voice-over: 'Gunshots — the leading cause of death among American teenagers.'

The voice-over becomes a face — a 35-year-old woman in funeral clothes. 'What happened to my sister's baby won't happen to mine. He is safe. He sleeps in a Bed-Box.'

Cut to Bed-Box.

'We start to go lighter here,' crop-hair said.

Male voice-over: '3/16 inch steel. Bullet proof. Fire resistant. Absolutely safe-sleep for your baby. The Bed-Box.'

Zoom into the Bed-Box to show a sleeping 5-year-old. The voice-over woman kneels to kiss her baby. She looks at the camera: '3/16 inch steel. I can sleep easy now . . . and so can my baby . . . in the Bed-Box.'

As the male voice-over read the ordering information on the screen, Angelo looked at the young woman next to him. She smiled up at him and nodded.

'You're right,' Angelo said. 'I think we've got a winner this time.'

THE HYENA-DEMOCRACY

At one time a group of hyenas had to move to a new territory because their old home was getting overcrowded and the food supply was short. Since they knew how to read — and were really quite proud of their accomplishments in this regard — they were surprised (but not necessarily unhappy) to find that the antelope who inhabited this new territory could not read at all. All they ever did was run about, leaping and bounding and looking very graceful.

'You mean, you can't read at all?' the chief hyena asked a young antelope who came leaping beautifully by.

'No. We've always liked jumping and leaping so much that we never learned how to read,' answered the antelope, who had politely stopped to reply.

'That is certainly no way to be,' said one hyena, who certainly wasn't that way. 'And it is certainly not civilized,' said another, as the civilized hyena finished eating the antelope, who now perhaps regretted that his mother had taught him to be polite to strangers who ask questions.

Since the hyenas were able to read and considered themselves civilized, they decided to elect a government — electing governments was in vogue at that time. And, of course, no one who was uncivilized and who could not read could vote. After all, there have be some reasonable qualifications to vote in a civilized country.

So the hyenas elected a parliament. And, naturally, as in all democratic countries where the qualified voters elect the government, the parliament passed laws that reflected the wishes of the voters. So the hyenas, who were never much in running and leaping, passed laws against running and leaping. 'Anybody who has done nothing wrong has nothing to run away from and leaping disturbs the peace' was the argument — which, of course, could not be logically refuted.

And since this was a democratic country that believed in a system of governmental checks and balances, the parliament turned the law over to the executive branch for enforcement. The hyena police soon arrested some antelope for running and leaping.

When the antelope were brought to trial, they were not very hopeful when they saw the hyena jury. But, since this was a democratic country in which the jury roles were filled by qualified voters, the antelope were not really very surprised. (What do antelope who can't read know about juries and trials, anyway?)

After the jury had convicted the antelope of running and leaping, the judge, who was also a hyena, suggested to the jury that they all go to dinner together to decide what the punishment should be. By the time the dinner was over — and all the antelope had been eaten — the judge and jury had decided that the punishment was for the antelope to be eaten (which, if you reflect on it for a minute, was quite a reasonable decision, everything considered).

As he pronounced the sentence, the judge gave a stirring little speech about democracy in which the qualified voters elect a parliament to pass the laws, and appoint a police force to enforce the laws, and set up a judicial system to pass judgment on lawbreakers. 'We are a democracy, and a democracy is a government of laws, not hyenas,' said the judge.

Moral: 'Hyena-democracy' is more attractive to hyenas than it is to antelope.

LITTLE RED RIDER FROM THE 'HOOD
(a children's story?)

She was called 'Little Red' because her mama, with her auburn hair, was called Red.

Red got that hair from her great granddaddy, an Irishman who 'climbed the tree' with Great Grandma. (Whether Grandma was willing or not, I never heard.)

Being Red Johnson is one thing but, to a man my age, being called 'Little Red' Rider is something else. (Once, I tried explaining my reaction to her name by comparing the original Red Rider with Hopalong Cassidy. But when she asked, 'Who's that?' I gave it up.) Anyway, her daddy's name was Bill Rider. Of course, that was before he converted.

After I got my VCR repaired and watched some of those movies from the '80s, I started teasing her about being 'Little Red Rider from the 'hood' — although I think she laughed at that just to be nice or, maybe (I have to admit), to get an extra-large tip that day.

But she was nice . . . at least, most of the time she was. And on my regular visits — in the afternoon on the second and fourth Thursdays — sometimes we'd just talk. In fact, usually, we'd just talk. And she'd tell me things. After we got to know each other, I think much of what she told me was true. . . .

One day, a few years back, Little Red was looking for a place to stay for a few days and, having no other choices left, she phoned her daddy's Aunt Lily. At first, the old woman sounded funny. But after some talk, Little Red was able to make connection and get her to say okay.

When Little Red arrived a few hours later, the door to Aunt Lily's house was opened by a man — big and tough-looking. He said his name was Bryan and he was a friend of 'Miss Lily.'

Since the man greeted her by name, Little Red accepted what he said. But as soon as she got in the house, she knew something was wrong. Aunt Lily was floating off to never-never land. Bryan, it turned out, was Aunt Lily's supplier. She would phone when she needed something and had some money. Then, when he could, he'd stop by.

At the big man's insistence, Little Red helped Aunt Lily into her bedroom. But then he blocked the door.

'Since you're here,' he said, 'Do you want some 'free' stuff?' . . . making it clear what he was going to get for 'free.'

'I don't want that . . . or you,' she said. But when he showed his big teeth in an un-funny smile, she knew she was in for it. So she let out a yell. Then he showed even more teeth . . . and came after her . . . with her yelling even more — and Aunt Lily still in never-never land.

But before he could catch her, the front door burst open and in came another man — just as big and obviously in better shape. Bryan turned to face him — 'Jason, what do you want?'

'I want nothing, Bryan. But I saw the girl come in and knew you were here. Then I heard the yelling.'

'This is none of your business,' Bryan said. 'You leave us be.'

'Not in Miss Lily's house,' Jason said. 'Some things just ain't right. You know that, Bryan.'

Anyway, the two men faced off for awhile . . . until Jason said, 'Bryan, if you just leave, I'll have no reason to say anything to anyone. But we're not going to have any foolishness today at Miss Lily's house.'

Bryan thought that over a bit and then, after telling Jason what would happen to him if he did say anything to anyone in the 'hood, he left.

Little Red Rider, of course, was very grateful to Jason . . . and showed it.

A week later, she was one of his main girls.

The following spring, I became one of her regulars — second and fourth Thursdays . . . in the afternoon. And Bryan still takes care of Miss Lily . . . when she has some money and he has time to stop by.

Note 8 - 'JUNETEENTH' — THE END OF SLAVERY

Slavery did not end when President Lincoln signed the Emancipation Proclamation on January 1, 1863; nor when Lee surrendered to Grant at Appomatox, Virginia, to end the Civil War on April 9, 1865. In fact, slavery did not cease until the Union army arrived in Galvaston, Texas, on June 19, 1865, over two months after the war ended. As the word spread across the state, 'Juneteenth' celebrations saluted freedom.

In modern times, 'Juneteenth' is observed throughout the nation.

NANCY WEBB WILLIAMS

As the first female or African American head of the Child Protective Services for Clark County (Las Vegas), Nevada, Nancy Webb Williams wrote poetry as 'Big Mama' to relieve the stress. A widow with three grown children, she accepted early retirement to devote her time to recording and retelling the 'old time' stories of black survival in a bigoted world, especially the humorous ones. *SWINGING ON THE PEARLY GATES*, her collection of 'retold' tales, is scheduled to be published by the University of Nevada Press. The author of four books of poetry, her latest is *THE SOUL SIDE - Big Mama Remembers* (1996).

THE HORSEFLY AND THE BLACK WIDOW SPIDER

A red-headed Horsefly, with rainbow colors in her gauzy wings, was out for a pleasure flight in the sun. Spying a Black Widow Spider repairing her spider web, the fly landed nearby for a chat.

'Good morning, Missus Widow,' said the Horsefly. ' It surely is one fine, beautiful morning.'

'That's what you say,' said the disgruntled Black Widow Spider; for the spider, being unused to the outdoors in the bright sunlight, was in a bad mood.

'I do, indeed, say,' said the Horsefly, tossing her red head while trying to make up her mind whether she should, or should not, take offense at the spider's poor attitude. But deciding there was nothing to be gained by taking offense at the spider's grumpiness, the Horsefly devised to turn the spider's bad mood into a moment of joy.

Whereupon, the fly, glowing inside herself for being such a good and helpful soul, spread her gauzy wings with their rainbow colors to let the spider enjoy the delightful spectacle of her beauty.

For all of the fly's good intentions, the spider did not stop weaving her web, not to so much as give the Horsefly a glance. Ignored, the Horsefly folded her wings annoyed.

And then in a raised voice of utter disgust, the Horsefly said, 'Missus Widow, I truly feel sorry for you. You are so unsocialized. Really, you are!'

Having caught the spider's attention with her angry outburst, the Horsefly patted her red head, then went on talking more softly.

'Perhaps you are unfriendly because you must spend your whole life looking like a dirty old hunk of soot with legs. It is a pity you let ugliness of one sort or another rule your life. You even creep around in the dark of night to escape being seen. And yet pretty is as pretty does. For it is said behind your back that you did away with your late husband because he found you less than comely. As if that would change your looks, or help you face your unpleasant disposition. And that disgusting web you spend so much time on! It wholly lacks the symmetry and beauty of your spider race . . .' The Horsefly paused to catch her breath and to pat her red head once again.

'What you say is true,' interrupted the Black Widow Spider, putting the last touches on her repaired web. 'While you, Missus Horsefly, seem to be as intelligent as you are beautiful. Truly, you possess a rare combination; for beauty seldom graces the brow of intelligence.'

'Yet I do not lack beauty, altogether.' the spider went on. 'I have a hidden beauty your eye cannot see from way up there where you sit, for on my abdomen is a rare and beautiful red diamond.'

'Now that I think of it,' said the Black Widow Spider scratching her head with a black, hairy leg, 'It's as if my red diamond were made to match the splendor of your lovely red head, Missus Fly.'

'Oh?' said the Horsefly, blushing until her red head fairly glowed scarlet. And yet there was a bit of disbelief showing in her voice, at the idea of the sooty spider owning anything of beauty.

'Yes,' said the Black Widow modestly, for the spider did not want to take any personal credit for the ownership of the diamond. 'It is a family heirloom passed down from generations past. If I do say so myself, it's crimson glow against my ebony body makes me look quite smart from the proper perspective.'

'It goes without saying, Missus Horsefly,' the spider said with convincing assertion, 'If it gives me a certain beauty, it will make you look simply gorgeous. Would you like to come down to try it on?'

Down flew the hapless Horsefly . . .

MORAL:
If we do not court flattery, flattery cannot harm us.

JOHN LITTLEJOHN AND THE TWO HEAVENS

(Author's note: We need a story . . . a story for our audience.

And we've got a great story to tell — many tales created by our ancestors, enslaved Africans, for telling and re-telling in the quarters to make life a little easier by making our people laugh.

These were 'our' stories of not-so-subtle slave resistance and, unlike the trickster-rabbit stories, never shared with white folks.

The hero of our story, John Littlejohn, was the best at everything that mattered to our people, but especially at shuckin' and jivin' and pulling the wool over Ol' Massa's eyes something awful.)

Ol' Massa see John Littlejohn choppin' in Ol' Miss' flower bed. Massa like to fun John Littlejohn, so he holler him, 'John. Oh, there, John! Come here, boy!' Ol' Massa say.

John Littlejohn s'pose to be weedin' 'round Ol' Miss' li'l pink flowers, but he be more'n happy to be stopped short by Ol' Massa.

'Yas suh, Massa.' John Littlejohn step lively, droppin' the hoe and mashin' four . . . five li'l pink flowers to a fare-you-well.

'John,' says Ol' Massa. 'Last night I had the strangest dream I ever dreamed. I'm going to tell you about it because you were in it, boy. Come on up here and sit down on the porch beside me. It's going to take me some time to tell you the whole thing,' Massa say. John Littlejohn climb onto the veranda 'n dropped right down at Massa's feet on the porch.

Then Ol' Massa go on with the story. 'I dreamed an angel came ... took me away to Colored Heaven. And me-oh-my, boy! There were all of these dilapidated shacks up there. Y'all's quarters here on the plantation look like mansions set next to those rickety, runned-down, loose-board shanties scattered around heaven for the colored.'

'And the streets! You should-a seen those streets, boy. They weren't gold like it's been said. No, huh-uh. Colored Heaven's got dirt-rut streets with big muddy holes in them ... big as pig wallows. And the smell! Stunk to high heaven!'

'And nowhere did I see any big shade trees. There were just a few scraggly, scrawny ol' switch-size trees up in Colored Heaven with a leaf or two dangling on the switches, here and there. I mean trees that couldn't throw any cool shade if they wanted to ... not at all like our big fine magnolias that throw enough shade for all of y'all to get under and have a fine picnic. Well, I nev- ...'

'Oh yes, another thing, before I forget, the heaven-gained colored saints didn't have haloes or wings or new shoes. In fact ... now listen to this, boy .. . those colored saints up there were as barefoot as the day they were born on earth.'

'But to tell you the truth, the colored didn't seem to mind one bit they didn't have heavenly accouterments or shade trees. They were singing their hearts out ... singing sweet praises to the Lord. Yes, indeed, they were, John, boy! And they were picking the Lord's cotton in a low cotton field that stretch so-o-o-o far off in the distance ... well, it must have ended in eternity.'

'Now what do you think of that dream, John, boy?' says Ol' Massa, with a mischief-grin on his face. 'Look at what the the Lord's got in mind for the colored folks who work hard and are good, obedient servants?'

'Hmmmm, Massa,' say John Littlejohn, studin' the story some in his mind.

'Yas, suh, Massa, reckon what you drempt must be so,' John say. 'The preacher 'n the saints always did say dreams come straight from the hand of God, so that dream of yo's must be so, Massa, even tho' it don't fit the picture of hebben in my head none.'

'But Massa,' John Littlejohn say, his spirits pickin' up some. 'It may be jus' one of them coincidence things, I reckon, but I had a dream las' night same as you, suh.' And John Littlejohn scratch his head on the bald spot where the dream was comin' back to him.

'You had a dream too?' says Ol' Massa. 'What did you dream, boy?'

'Massa, suh, I done dreamt a angel snuck this here cullud boy into white hebben. Showed this cullud boy all the glory whut the culluds goin' miss. And, Massa, white hebben be a beautiful place! Yas suh, glorify place.'

'The streets in white hebben be full carat gold with sparkly jewels studded all in them. And there be crusted jewels in the gold cobble sidewalks for the good white folks to walk on in they gold hebben shoes 'n slippers. And there be big ... I mean B-I-G ... shade trees yonder to keep the good white folks plenty

63

cool.'

'And, Massa, lots of flowers be everywhere makin' the white hebben air smell so sweet 'n nice. And, too, God got the prettiest, greenest, carpet-smooth grass all 'round y'all's hebben. White hebben be jus' like a picture on the wall, Massa.'

'Ain't nary a fly, skeeter, snake ... none of them pesky critters in white hebben to bother y'all good white folks. There be pretty ponds of water there. And streams ...'

'And Massa, mansions be everywhere! Big mansions, brick, stone all the bes' made everything. One mansion be more beautiful than the nex' with big white columns, archin' trees, verandys 'n all sech as that. Them mansions be sech as to make y'alls grand plantation houses look like the sorry cullud shacks on slave row, Ohhh, Massa, white hebben be the grandest, mos' beautiful place God ever made any time, any where.'

'But one thing 'bout it, Massa. There warn't no peoples there. Not nary a soul!'

EDITOR'S NOTE ABOUT THE NOTES

The factual information used in the various notes in this anthology came from the following sources on my book shelves. (The interpretations of the information are my own.) The bibliography is presented in chronological order of first publication.

THE CONSTITUTION OF THE UNITED STATES.

NARRATIVE OF THE LIFE OF FREDERICK DOUGLASS AN AMERICAN SLAVE WRITTEN BY HIMSELF (first published in Boston in 1845).

THE SABLE ARM: Black Troops in the Union Army, 1861-1865, by Dudley Taylor Cornish (Lawrence, KS: University Press of Kansas, 1956).

A DOCUMENTARY HISTORY OF THE NEGRO PEOPLE IN THE UNITED STATES, edited by Herbert Aptheker (New York: The Citadel Press, 1969).

THE AMISTAD AFFAIR, by Christopher Martin (New York: Tower Publications, 1970).

BLACK WOMEN IN WHITE AMERICA: A Documentary History, edited by Gerda Lerner (New York: Vantage Books, 1972).

BULLWHIP DAYS: The Slaves Remember, an oral history, edited by James Mellon. (New York: Avon Books, 1988).

NOW IS YOUR TIME! The African-American Struggle for Freedom, by Walter Dean Myers (New York: HarperCollins Publishers, 1991).

I, TOO, SING AMERICA The African American Book of Days, by Paula L. Woods and Felix H. Liddell (New York: Workman Publishing, 1992).

1001 THINGS EVERYONE SHOULD KNOW ABOUT AFRICAN AMERICAN HISTORY, by Jeffery C. Stewart (New York: Doubleday, 1996).